FULL-SCALE TIME WAR

"You will have the unenviable mission of trying to determine whether or not we're dealing with a massive timestream split, Mr. Delaney," Forrester said. "If that's the case, then there's a good possibility that the people from that second timeline are conducting some sort of subversive action on the northwest frontier of the British Raj. Your job is to determine who they are and stop them."

"And if we can't?" Delaney said.

"Then we may wind up with a full-scale time war between two parallel timelines," Forrester said. "Apparently the first shot of that war has already been fired in the Khyber Pass."

The Time Wars Series by Simon Hawke

THE KHYBER CONNECTION

SIMON HAWKE

ACE SCIENCE FICTION BOOKS
NEW YORK

This book is an Ace Science
Fiction original edition, and has never
been previously published.

THE KHYBER CONNECTION

An Ace Science Fiction Book / published by arrangement with
the author

PRINTING HISTORY
Ace Science Fiction edition / October 1986

ISBN: 0-441-43725-7

Ace Science Fiction Books are published by
The Berkley Publishing Group,
200 Madison Avenue, New York, New York 10016.
PRINTED IN THE UNITED STATES OF AMERICA

A CHRONOLOGICAL
HISTORY OF
THE TIME WARS

April 1, 2425:   Dr. Wolfgang Mensinger invents the chronoplate at the age of 115, discovering time travel. Later he would construct a small scale working prototype for use in laboratory experiments specially designed to avoid any possible creation of a temporal paradox. He is hailed as the "Father of Temporal Physics."

July 14, 2430:   Mensinger publishes "There Is No Future," in which he redefines relativity, proving that there is no such thing as *the* future, but an infinite number of potential future scenarios which are absolute relative only to their present. He also announces the discovery of "non-specific time" or temporal limbo, later known as "the dead zone."

October 21, 2440:   Wolfgang Mensinger dies. His son, Albrecht, perfects the chronoplate and carries on the work, but loses control of the discovery to political interests.

June 15, 2460:	Formation of the international Committee for Temporal Intelligence, with Albrecht Mensinger as director. Specially trained and conditioned "agents" of the committee begin to travel back through time in order to conduct research and field test the chronoplate apparatus. Many become lost in transition, trapped in the limbo of nonspecific time known as "the dead zone." Those who return from successful temporal voyages often bring back startling information necessitating the revision of historical records.
March 22, 2461:	*The Consorti Affair*—Cardinal Lodovico Consorti is excommunicated from the Roman Catholic Church for proposing that agents travel back through time to obtain empirical evidence that Christ arose following His crucifixion. The Consorti Affair sparks extensive international negotiations amidst a volatile climate of public opinion concerning the proper uses for the new technology. Temporal excursions are severely curtailed. Concurrently, espionage operatives of several nations infiltrate the Committee for Temporal Intelligence.
May 1, 2461:	Dr. Albrecht Mensinger appears before a special international conference in Geneva, composed of political leaders and members of the scientific community. He attempts to alleviate fears about the possible misuses of time travel. He further refuses to cooperate with any attempts at militarizing his father's discovery.

February 3, 2485:	The research facilities of the Committee for Temporal Intelligence are seized by troops of the TransAtlantic Treaty Organization.
January 25, 2492:	The Council of Nations meets in Buenos Aires, capital of the United Socialist States of South America, to discuss increasing international tensions and economic instability. A proposal for "an end to war in our time" is put forth by the chairman of the Nippon Conglomerate Empire. Dr. Albrecht Mensinger, appearing before the body as nominal director of the Committee for Temporal Intelligence, argues passionately against using temporal technology to resolve international conflicts, but cannot present proof that the past can be affected by temporal voyagers. Prevailing scientific testimony reinforces the conventional wisdom that the past is an immutable absolute.
December 24, 2492:	Formation of the Referee Corps, brought into being by the Council of Nations as an extranational arbitrating body with sole control over temporal technology and authority to stage temporal conflicts as "limited warfare" to resolve international disputes.
April 21, 2493:	On the recommendation of the Referee Corps, a subordinate body named the Observer Corps is formed, taking over most of the functions of the Committee for Temporal Intelligence, which is redesignated as the Temporal Intelligence Agency. Under the aegis of the Council of Nations and the Referee Corps, the TIA absorbs

the intelligence agencies of the world's governments and is made solely answerable to the Referee Corps. Dr. Mensinger resigns his post to found the Temporal Preservation League, a group dedicated to the abolition of temporal conflict.

June, 2497–
March, 2502:

Referee Corps presides over initial temporal confrontation campaigns, accepting "grievances" from disputing nations, selecting historical conflicts of the past as "staging grounds" and supervising the infiltration of modern troops into the so-called "cannon fodder" ranks of ancient warring armies. Initial numbers of temporal combatants are kept small, with infiltration facilitated by cosmetic surgery and implant conditioning of soldiers. The results are calculated based upon successful return rate and a complicated "point spread." Soldiers are monitored via cerebral implants, enabling Search & Retrieve teams to follow their movements and monitor mortality rate. The media dubs temporal conflicts the "Time Wars."

2500–2510:

Extremely rapid growth of massive support industry catering to the exacting art and science of temporal conflict. Rapid improvements in international economic climate follows, with significant growth in productivity and rapid decline in unemployment and inflation rate. There is a gradual escalation of the Time Wars with the majority of the world's armed services converting to temporal duty status.

Growth of the Temporal Preservation League as a peace movement with an intensive lobby effort and mass demonstrations against the Time Wars. Mensinger cautions against an imbalance in temporal continuity due to the increasing activity of the Time Wars.

September 2, 2514: Mensinger publishes his "Theories of Temporal Relativity," incorporating his solution to the Grandfather Paradox and calling once again for a ceasefire in the Time Wars. The result is an upheaval in the scientific community and a hastily reconvened Council of Nations to discuss his findings, leading to the Temporal Strategic Arms Limitations Talks of 2515.

March 15, 2515– June 1, 2515: T-SALT held in New York City. Mensinger appears before the representatives at the sessions and petitions for an end to the Time Wars. A ceasefire resolution is framed, but tabled due to lack of agreement among the members of the Council of Nations. Mensinger leaves the T-SALT a broken man.

November 18, 2516: Dr. Albrecht Mensinger experiences total nervous collapse shortly after being awarded the Benford Prize.

December 25, 2516: Dr. Albrecht Mensinger commits suicide. Violent demonstrations by members of the Temporal Preservation League.

January 1, 2517: Militant members of the Temporal Preservation League band together to form the Timekeepers, a terrorist offshoot of the League, dedicated to the complete destruction of the war machine. They announce their presence to the world by assassinating three members of the Referee Corps and bombing the Council of Nations meeting in Buenos Aires, killing several heads of state and injuring many others.

September 17, 2613: Formation of the First Division of the U.S. Army Temporal Corps as a crack commando unit following the successful completion of a "temporal adjustment" involving the first serious threat of a timestream split. The First Division, assigned exclusively to deal with threats to temporal continuity, is designated as "the Time Commandos."

PROLOGUE ════════

When you're wounded an' left on Afghanistan's plains,
An' the women come out to cut up your remains,
Just roll to your rife an' blow out your brains,
An' go to your Gawd like a soldier.

Rudyard Kipling

The name Hindu Kush meant "Hindu Killer." To the foreigner who had grown up with the myth that Hell was located far beneath the surface of the earth, the Hindu Kush was proof it could be found at the top of the world as well. The 700-mile-long wall of rock that bordered Afghanistan on the north lay to the west of the impassable Himalayas. The terrain was otherworldly, both in its savage beauty and in its forboding deadliness, a rock-strewn, broken landscape which looked as if it had been carved out of the earth with Vulcan's chisel. For six months out of every year a banshee winter wind known as the *shamal* screamed down ice-encrusted slopes that made the Grand Canyon look like a small Arizona drywash. During the summer months the heat defied belief. Here and there could be found a small oasis, lush and verdant, a valley rich with fig palms and walnut groves, but for the most part it was a trackless wasteland of sheer rock which ripped holes in the sky.

The country had defied the armies of Darius the Great and Alexander. The Mongol hordes of Genghis Khan and Tamerlane had stormed through its mountain passes, but had never truly conquered it. The British Raj had floundered here for years, arrogantly claiming it as part of its empire, yet never taming it. The country, and the wild people who inhabited its inhospitable heights, endured and would not be subjugated. The Hindu Kush killed all those who did not belong there. It was a cold and lonely place to die.

Huddled behind an outcropping of rock in one of the countless hairpin turns of the Khyber Pass, Sergeant Thomas Court struggled to hold on to life and prayed the Ghazis would not find him. His body was pierced by three jezail bullets, but he did not fear dying of his wounds so much as he feared the ministrations of the Ghazis. He could hear the screams of other wounded soldiers as the Afridi tribesmen found them and proceeded with the vivisection. The throat-rending screams echoed off the rock walls of the Khyber like the ululation of the damned in Dante's final circle. The mountain tribes showed no mercy to the *firinghi* invader.

Court had managed to half crawl, half drag himself up into the rocks, where he had taken refuge in a small stone *sangar*, an improvised fortification of piled boulders which tribesmen constructed for use as sniper's nests. There were hundreds of them in the pass, at varying elevations, and from these primitive stone bunkers the Pathans would fire down at those below them with their jezails—the long-barreled matchlock rifles they employed with devastating accuracy, able to drop a British soldier at a distance of 1000 yards. Their skill with the primitive jezails made them that much more formidable with captured British Martini-Henry and Snider rifles, superior firearms which the tribesmen turned against their original owners with unholy glee.

The scene below where Court lay in the *sangar*, resembled a painting by Heironymous Bosch. Bodies were scattered everywhere. British soldiers and khaki-clad Sikhs of the Indian Army, Gurkhas, kilted Highlanders, corpses torn and bloodied, pack animals wandering about untended, riderless horses, camels oblivious to the death throes all around them; it was a scene of mind-numbing carnage through which the ghostly, white-clad Ghazis moved like wraiths, brandishing their *charra* knives. The grisly, swordlike blades rose and fell on those luckless enough to have survived. As the hour grew late, the screams became fewer, though no less hideous.

Court shivered and cursed the sadists in the Referee Corps who had selected this particular horror as an historical scenario within which to stage a temporal confrontation action. He had survived the trench fighting of the First World War, been wounded in a naval action off the Barbary Coast, and had made it back from the death march at Bataan. He had served as a Roman legionary, an Indian scout in the American southwest, and a Spanish conquistador under Pizarro, but nothing in his career as a soldier in the Temporal Army Corps could compare with this bone-chilling nightmare. Nothing he had ever seen had terrified him as much as the sight of hundreds of screaming Ghazis pouring down out of the rocks, descending upon the regiment like locusts under the black flags of the jehad. Never before had he encountered fighters like the Ghazis. When the Pathan tribes went Ghazi, it made no difference whether they were Afridi or Mohmand or Yusufzai. Any feuds between the Orakzais of Tirah and the Mahsuds of Waziristan became forgotten as they united in jehad and became Ghazi, Muslim fanatics in the grip of a religious fever, kamikazes without planes who believed that the slaughter of the infidels would open up the gates of paradise to them. With such an incentive, they knew no fear. They could not be turned. The blessings of the Prophet were upon them, and death in combat was but a passage to Islamic heaven. The British soldiers had fought bravely, but they were outnumbered ten to one. They had been softened up by sniper fire and rock bombardment from the cliffs, and then the human wave engulfed them and they died. And died. And died.

Court held onto his Martini-Henry as if the rifle were his lover. He had one round left. Only one. If the Ghazis found him, he would write his own name on that bullet. If they didn't find him, if he could hang on long enough, the Search and Retrieve teams would clock in from the 27th century and home in on his implant. If he was still alive then, they would clock him back to his own time and he would be treated for his wounds in an army hospital. The referees would then add his survival into the point spread that would guide them in reaching a decision in the arbitration action that had sent him back to the year 1897, to fight in a war within a war. If he survived, he would never know who won. He would never know how many other soldiers of the 27th century had died in the Khyber Pass, slaughtered by the Ghazis. He would never even know the details of the events in his own time which had led to the arbitration action. He would only know that he had survived, that he had beaten the odds in a game in which the mortality rate was astronomical. He would know that he had survived to fight again and that the next time, perhaps, the odds would finally catch up to him. Maybe they already had.

He thought about his one remaining bullet. His entire life began to revolve around that tiny piece of lead.

It was growing dark. Vultures wheeled overhead. Court's teeth were chattering. His wounds no longer pained him. He knew that was a bad sign. There was nothing he could do. There were no longer any screams coming from below him. Nothing lived down there. The Ghazis had melted away into the mountains, taking with them the spoils of the battle—the guns, supplies, and animals. He had been spared death by dismemberment, but now it seemed only a matter of what would kill him first—exposure or his wounds. He thought about that precious bullet. It was a tempting thought, a secure and quick solution. Yet, on the other hand, the instinct to survive was strong within him. The S & R teams would arrive soon, they had to. Like the mythic Valkyries, they would bear away the bodies of the dead soldiers from the future and sweep the battlefield to check for possible survivors. All he had to do was stay alive.

He heard a flutter of wings. Large wings. For a moment he thought he was hallucinating. It seemed entirely too melodramatic to be dying in a mountain pass, in a savage wilderness at the ceiling of the world, and to hear the flapping of the deathbird's wings approaching. And it was a deathbird, only a prosaic one, a vulture. The ugly bird alighted on the *sangar* wall not two feet away. Its scrofulous face stared at him indifferently.

"Beat it, damn you," Court said. "I'm not dead yet."

The ugly bird opened and closed its beak with a snap, as if to say, "That's okay, I'll wait."

Court pegged a rock at it and missed, but the vulture vacated its perch above him with an irate squawk. He heard the rock bouncing down the slope, starting a brief, miniature avalanche as it dislodged smaller stones which skittered down with a pattering sound, and then all was still again. But only for a moment. Court froze as he heard the sounds of somebody or something climbing up the slope towards him. It could be animal or man. Please, thought Court, let it be an animal, even a hungry tiger, anything but a Ghazi tribesman. He only had one bullet. It might be enough to stop one Ghazi, but its sound could bring others. He lay perfectly still, afraid to move, unable to. He heard the sound of labored breathing.

His sweaty hands clenched around the stock of his rifle, bringing it around in front of him, bayonet pointed toward the sound. The white-robed figure stepped into view. Court held his breath. The face beneath the turban was in shadow, but as the Ghazi turned toward him, Court gasped involuntarily. The moonlight revealed the dark skin of an Afridi tribesman, but the features were his own. In the same instant, his doppelganger's breath hissed out and he muttered a most un-Islamic oath.

"Sweet Jesus!"

Half convinced he was delirious, Court kept the rifle pointed at the apparition and said, "Who are you?"

The Ghazi stared at him. "Thomas Court," he said. "Sergeant, U.S. Army Temporal Corps."

"Yes, I'm Court, but how—" and somehow he suddenly knew that the man had not recognized him, but rather had answered his question. Just as suddenly, he realized the man was going to kill him. They both fired at the same time. The echoes of their shots rolled against the rock walls of the Khyber Pass and died away in stillness.

1

Colonel Moses Forrester, commander of the First Division of the United States Army Temporal Corps, was unaccustomed to wearing his full dress uniform in his own quarters, but the status of his visitor demanded it. It was the first time Forrester had ever met face to face with the director general of the Referee Corps. If the fact of the meeting was unusual in itself, the circumstances of it were even more so. The meeting was top secret and there were armed guards stationed outside in the corridor and by the lift tubes. The entire floor of the Command Staff BOQ where Forrester was quartered had been sealed off, and the other officers billeted there had been given orders to be elsewhere between 1900 and 2100 hours. The director general had been supplied with the coordinates to clock directly into Forrester's living room. He arrived with his personal bodyguards, who took up stations just inside the entrance to the living room and in the foyer, by the front door.

The man who merited such treatment was thin and

frail, his aged face deeply lined, his head bald, like Forrester's. He wore a simple, two-piece white suit with the small gold and platinum medallion of his office worn as an amulet around his neck. Compared to Forrester's bull-like physique, the director general's frame looked emaciated, but his light gray eyes were bright with vitality and intelligence.

"Colonel Forrester, I'm pleased to meet you. I am Director General Vargas." His voice was soft and low, with a flowing, soothing quality.

"Sir!" said Forrester, snapping to attention. "This is an honor."

Vargas nodded once, accepting the compliment. "Please, Colonel, stand at ease. We shall dispense with protocol henceforth. We have important matters to discuss. Do sit down."

Forrester waited until Vargas sat down on the couch before he took the chair opposite, across the low glass coffee table. "May I offer you anything, sir?"

"No, thank you," Vargas said. "I will come right to the point. The conversation we are about to have is, of course, classified."

"I understand, sir."

"Which personnel make up your best historical adjustment team?" said Vargas.

Forrester replied without hesitation. "That would be my executive officer, Lieutenant Colonel Lucas Priest; Lieutenant Finn Delaney, and Sergeant Andre Cross."

Vargas pursed his lips and nodded. "If we may speak candidly, strictly off the record, I would like to ask you some questions about these personnel."

"Certainly, sir."

"Their record speaks for itself, yet I am struck by the incongruity of Lieutenant Colonel Priest's being a model officer and Lieutenant Delaney's disciplinary record."

Forrester said nothing.

"You have no response?" said Vargas.

"I'm waiting for a question, sir."

Vargas smiled. "How very diplomatic of you, Colonel. Very well, then. How is it that the finest officer under your command is teamed with a man who has one of the worst records of offenses in the entire Temporal Corps, a man who in civilian life might well have been a convicted felon?"

"With all due respect, sir," said Forrester, "there is absolutely no evidence to support such a conclusion. Granted, Lieutenant Delaney has a disastrous disciplinary record. Calling him a maverick would be a gross understatement. However, I would like to point out that every one of his disciplinary offenses occurred in Plus Time, not in the field on the Minus side. And, frankly, I am far more concerned with his performance in the field. I would also like to underscore the nature of those offenses."

"Drunk and disorderly," said Vargas. "Numerous incidences of direct disobedience to specific orders. Even more numerous incidences of striking superior officers. Insubordination. Etcetera, etcetera."

"Exactly my point, sir," said Forrester, wondering where the discussion was leading. The director general was clearly familiar with the records. The question was, why should he have taken the trouble? What could possibly be so important that the director general of the Referee Corps would personally review the dossiers of an adjustment team?

"I don't dispute that Lieutenant Delaney holds the record for the most reductions in grade of any soldier in the Temporal Corps," he continued. "But that's only looking at it one way. He also holds the record for the most promotions for outstanding service in the field. There are soldiers, such as Lieutenant Colonel Priest, who possess qualities and temperaments that make them excellent officers in the field as well as on the parade ground, if you follow my meaning.''

Vargas nodded.

"Others, such as Lieutenant Delaney, possess qualities and temperaments that clash violently with the exigencies of the military infrastructure.'' Forrester paused. "This does not necessarily make them bad soldiers. In some cases these are people whose abilities are underutilized, who possess personality traits that result in their being suffocated by military bureaucracy. Their personalities render it difficult, if not impossible, for them to follow the orders of officers who are superior to them only in rank. Yet at the same time, these are people who would be even less comfortable in civilian life. They are soldiers first and foremost. In the proper role, and with the right commander, they can excel.''

"Meaning no offense, Colonel,'' Vargas said, "but are you quite certain such a description fits Lieutenant Delaney?''

"Like a glove, sir. You can't take a man like Delaney and put him behind a desk. He's a veteran of numerous temporal campaigns. If you demand parade ground spit and polish of him, and expect him to jump like a monkey on a stick every time some light colonel half his age says "Boo,'' you have a ripe candidate for a court-martial. On the other hand if you put him in the field where he belongs and give him an opportunity to show initiative, you have a T. E. Lawrence or an Otto Skorzeny. If Delaney wasn't worth his weight in gold as a commando, I'd have had his ass a long time ago—begging your pardon, sir. The fact that he coldcocks an occasional first lieutenant fresh out of OCS, or gets into a drunken barroom brawl, is of less interest to me than the fact that he's a first-rate soldier when the chips are down. You can't take a fighting cock and put him in a henhouse and expect him to lay eggs. If I want a man in the field calling the shots, I'll pick Priest. If I want someone at my back, I'll take Delaney. If I can have them both, I'll bring you results, as their record shows.''

Vargas smiled. "A most impressive argument, Colonel. According to the records, you have interceded for Lieutenant Delaney in almost every case. I was curious to hear your reasons."

"And having heard them?" said Forrester.

"Having heard them, I am satisfied," said Vargas. "Which brings us to the third member of this team, Sergeant Cross. Her dossier makes for truly remarkable reading. A 12th century woman relocated to the present and programmed with a modern education. Fascinating. Official records aside, however, what is your personal opinion of her?"

Forrester smiled. "Frankly, sir, if I were seventy years younger, I'd be tempted to take a highly personal interest in Sergeant Cross. She's sharp, quick thinking, possesses a high degree of initiative, and is utterly fearless. She grew up an orphan in the 12th century, totally disadvantaged, yet she managed to become literate, at least by the standards of her time, and to survive in a hostile society. She fights as well as any man and better than most. She's highly adaptable, so much so that she can, and has, easily passed as a man in male-dominated societies. She is the only case of Plus Time temporal relocation on record, and the fact that she is where she is speaks for itself in regard to her abilities. The three of them together function as a well-integrated whole. Whatever it is they are being considered for, sir, I can give them my unqualified endorsement, but I can tell you right now that I'd fight like hell against having them removed from under my command. I'd stake my life on those three. In fact, I have.''

"Excellent," said Vargas. "I am satisfied that we have selected the right people for the job. I merely wanted to reassure myself by speaking with you, because this time a great deal more than just your life may depend on their performance, Colonel. If they fail, we may *all* die."

The mission briefing was held in Forrester's quarters, not in one of the briefing rooms, as was usually the case. Forrester's orderly was not present. There were only the four of them. The three commandos were dressed in black Temporal Army base fatigues, bare except for their insignia of rank on narrow black armbands and their division insignia, a stylized number 1 bisected by the symbol of infinity, pinned to their collars. Forrester was still wearing his full dress uniform, having sent for them immediately following the director general's departure. Since their commander always dressed in black base fatigues and never wore his many decorations, the sight of him in what Delaney referred to as "full goose turnout" had their curiosity aroused.

They sat around the table, drinking coffee, while Forrester stood. It was not unusual for them to sit in the presence of their commanding officer. Forrester preferred to stand while conducting briefings, so that he could pace back and forth, a practice he claimed helped him think more clearly.

Lucas Priest somehow managed to look as if he were sitting erect, even while he leaned back against the sofa cushions. His fatigues were crisply pressed and his dark brown hair neatly combed. He was slender and fit, the perfect incarnation of an officer and a gentleman. His left eye was natural, his right bionic, though not even the closest physical inspection would have revealed the difference.

Andre Cross was a tall young woman with straw-blonde hair. Her outward symmetry belied the fact that she possessed unusually broad shoulders for a female, her uniform masking her extremely well-developed muscularity. She was more striking than attractive, with the graceful poise of a natural athlete and a calm self-assurance in her bearing.

By contrast, Finn Delaney had the outward appearance of a lout. The burly, redheaded Irishman had the physique and posture of a bear and a face that seemed constantly on the verge of an insolent grin, even when he was serious. His uniform looked as if he had slept in it—he often did—and the top of his blouse was unfastened, as usual, revealing a massive and thickly corded neck. In any other unit he would have been a walking invitation to be placed on report. He had spent his entire adult life in the service, a testimony more to obstinacy than to aptitude, but after years of serving on the front lines in the regular corps in battles throughout time, he had finally found a commander who understood how to put his unique capabilities to use.

"What I am about to tell you is classified information," said Forrester. "You will report to mission programming directly following this briefing and clock out to your assignment from there. There is to be no discussion of this mission with anyone, repeat, anyone outside this room. Clear?"

"Yes, sir," they said.

"I have just concluded a meeting with the director general of the Referee Corps," Forrester said. Even Delaney sat up. "He has personally reviewed your dossiers, which should give you some indication of the gravity of this situation. I'll make it brief. Recently an arbitration action was conducted in Afghanistan in the year 1897, during the Pathan revolt. Background of the conflict between the British Raj and the frontier mountain tribesmen is as follows:

"The British annexed the Punjab territory to their Indian Empire in the year 1849. The move was predicated upon what Britain referred to as her 'Forward Policy,' which entailed a gradual extension and consolidation of British influence into the frontier, chiefly to create a so-called "buffer state" between the British Raj in India and what was considered to be likely Russian expansionism. British military campaigns in the Hindu Kush range of Afghanistan resulted partly from concern that Russian control of the area would give them a direct invasion route into India and partly from a desire to pacify the region and curtail invasions into the Punjab of plundering mountain tribesmen. The Pathan tribes recognized no law other than their own and that of the Koran, as imparted to them by tribal holy men who frequently used it to serve their own purposes.

"In the years following the annexation, the Royal Indian Army conducted over fifty punitive campaigns against the Pathans, a situation complicated by there being some half a dozen major independent Pathan tribes on the frontier and dozens of smaller Pathan groups who either gave their allegiance to one of the larger tribes, or to the British, or fought amongst themselves, depending on what side of the bed they got out of that morning. With so many armed conflicts going on, it was decided that the period made a good scenario for conducting temporal arbitration actions.

"During one such campaign, Search and Retrieve units clocked in following a battle between soldiers of the Royal Indian Army and Afridi tribesmen. In recovering the bodies of temporal soldiers who had been infiltrated into the British ranks, S & R found the body of one Sergeant Thomas Court. Court had apparently dragged himself up into the rocks to hide from Ghazi tribesmen who were butchering the wounded. Found next to him was the body of an Afridi tribesman. They evidently killed each other. Now here's where it gets interesting.

"With the exception of clothing and coloring, the two bodies were alike in virtually every respect. As he was dying, Court had assumed a curious posture with the index finger of his right hand pressed up against his temple and his other hand pointing at the head of the dead tribesmen. The S & R team leader realized Court had tried to leave a message. He thought Court might have been attempting to indicate an implant in the body of his twin, but their scan did not reveal one. Despite that, the team leader took a gamble and risked clocking back with both bodies so that an investigation could be conducted. An autopsy revealed the presence of an implant, but it was calibrated to a different frequency than standard Temporal Corps implants, which is why S & R's scanning equipment didn't register it. More significantly, both bodies had the same fingerprints and the same retinal patterns. A thorough biochemical analysis revealed that the two bodies were identical right down to the DNA. *They were both the same man.*"

"That isn't possible," said Delaney. "That would involve a temporal paradox."

"Which is precisely why the findings were checked several times and then reported directly to the Referee Corps," said Forrester. "There was no question. Moreover, the dark pigmentation of the dead Afridi's skin and the slightly larger nose were both discovered to be the result of minor cosmetic surgery procedures. Both bodies were Thomas Court."

"That's crazy," Lucas Priest said. "There has to be some mistake."

"The results were checked and rechecked," said Forrester. "There's no doubt. The Referee Corps has determined that two possibilities exist that might explain this situation. You're not going to like either one of them.

The first possible explanation is that someone has figured out a way to alter implant signals and is experimenting with a procedure meant to sabotage temporal conflicts by somehow programming individuals to carry out certain tasks. In the case of Court the theory is that someone might have gotten their hands on him in Plus Time and brainwashed him into going back into the past, programmed to kill 'himself' while he was involved in a temporal campaign. A sort of test case. Since both Courts died at the same time, or at roughly the same time, temporal paradox was avoided. Or perhaps the brainwashed Court, assuming that was the case, would have died upon clocking back to Plus Time, in which event the end result would have been the same."

"It could be possible," Delaney said. "We experimented with similar problem modules in RCS and determined that it could happen, theoretically. Only this isn't theory. I can think of only one other possible explanation. A timestream split."

"Precisely," said Forrester. "I told you that you wouldn't like it. If a timestream split has occurred, there are no indications to show at *what point* it occurred. In that case, the fact of a non-standard implant indicates something even more frightening. If a timestream split has gone down, assuming the people in the parallel timeline are aware of it, then their entire existence depends upon that split."

"Which means they have to prevent us from adjusting it," said Andre.

"Exactly," Forrester said. "The second Thomas Court could have been from that second timeline, a parallel universe created by an historical disruption. There is a possibility that in spite of our defeating Drakov during our battle with the Time Pirates, a split might still have occurred, but the Referee Corps has determined that clocking back to that battle would be too hazardous. We barely got through that one by the skin of our teeth, and trying to go back to it again would increase the odds of creating even more temporal splits. And there's no way of determining if that particular scenario was the cause. It could have occurred in any of a dozen temporal campaigns, or hundreds, or even thousands. Without knowing for certain, no standard adjustment operation can be attempted.''

''With all due respect, sir,'' said Delaney, ''if that's the case, what the hell are we supposed to do?''

''You will have the unenviable mission of trying to determine whether or not we're dealing with a massive timestream split, Mr. Delaney,'' Forrester said. ''If that's the case, then there's a good possibility that people from that second timeline are conducting some sort of subversive action on the northwest frontier of the British Raj. If, in fact, that's what we're faced with, then the Time Wars are about to be escalated into an entirely new dimension. The people from the parallel timeline will be trying to interfere with our history in order to preserve their own. Your job is to find out who they are and stop them.''

''And if we can't?'' Delaney said.

''Then we may wind up with a full-scale time war between two parallel timelines,'' Forrester said. ''Apparently the first shot of that war has already been fired in the Khyber Pass.''

2

The city of Peshawar in the Kashmir was the point where the trade routes from China, Turkestan, and Persia intersected. Its colorful bazaar was a cacophany of Bokhara rug dealers, Chinese silk merchants, almond growers from the valleys of the Hindu Kush, horse breeders from Turkestan, brass and silver merchants, fruit sellers and pilgrims on their way to Mecca. The square teemed with beggars and fakirs; charm sellers and holy men; Afridis from the Khyber Pass armed with jezail rifles and long knives; white-robed Afghanis from Kabul, gray-clad Orakzais from the Bolan, and mysterious, wraithlike Kashmiri women cloaked in veils and silks; all intermingling beneath the white-stone minarets of the mosque of Mahabat Khan. British Royal Cavalry rode with tack jingling and banners rippling in the wind through packed streets where Mongol hordes once left their hoofprints.

To the northwest of the city lay the Khyber Pass, the most direct route east into India. The Khyber was only thirty miles long, but it was like a jagged crack through solid walls of rock, a twisting, turning gorge above which towered sheer cliffs that seemed to stretch up into eternity.

The people who lived there were as wild as the country they inhabited. They ceaselessly fought foreign invaders and each other, governed only by the Koran and the Pakhtunwali, their unwritten laws of social conduct, which were composed of three main dictums. Melmastia demanded that anyone who crossed the threshold of a Pathan dwelling be treated as an honored guest, even a sworn enemy. Nanawatai dictated that asylum must be granted to anyone who sought it, whether it was a fugitive from foreigners—*firinghi*—or from other Pathans. And Badal, the strictest commandment of them all, called for revenge, payment taken in blood for any wrong done to a Pathan, any personal affront, any infringement of those things most precious to a mountain tribesman: *zar, zan,* and *zamin*—gold, women, and land.

Into this country and into their domain came the British Royal Indian Army, prepared to pit its might against a half dozen rebellious mountain tribes. In the north there were the Mohmands and the Yusufzais in the mountains of Bajaur, Buner, Dir, and Swat. In the Khyber Pass there were the Afridis. The domain of the Orakzais was in the high mountain valleys of Tirah, country they shared uneasily with several Afridi tribes. In Waziristan and Bannu, to the south, were the Mahsuds and the Waziris. Come to pacify their region were Gordon Highlanders and Gurkha regiments; Sikhs and Punjabi Muslims in the Queen's Own Corps of Guides; the renowned native Khyber Rifles; seasoned British infantrymen and young, green subalterns sent to reinforce the edicts of the government, or Sirkar, with the strong arm of the Raj, with the dreaded curved *kukri* of the Gurkhas and the Martini-Henry rifles of the British in fantry. They came with Hindu infantry called *sepoys* and with Indian cavalrymen called *sowars*. They came with saddle-mounted guns called *zomboruks* and French Maxim machine guns. They came with mules and camels, horses and attendants, cooks, mahout elephant drivers, stewards, *bhisti* water carriers, and supplies. And unknown to any of them, they came with three commandos from the 27th century.

Finn Delaney was dressed in the khaki uniform of a subaltern in the 11th Bengal Lancers, while Lucas Priest and Andre Cross were attired in civilian clothing, their cover being that of a Christian missionary and his nurse. The setup would allow them considerable flexibility, as the Bengal Lancers were a highly mobile regiment, and Christian missionaries, while having extremely limited success in converting adherents to Islam, were welcome among the mountain tribes for setting up hospitals and providing basic medical care, which was otherwise nonexistent. The three of them strolled through the bazaar, examining the multitude of weapons on display in the cloth-covered booths. Curved swords called *tulwars* gleamed in the bright sunlight. Jazail rifles were on display side by side with local imitations of British ordnance such as the "Brown Bess" muskets, and even copies of the Snider rifle. Knives of all lengths and styles were to be had cheaply, as was hashish, smoked in small water pipes called chillums. Arrack, an alcoholic drink distilled from rice, was offered for refreshment along with a hemp infusion known as bhang. *Risaldars,* Indian cavalry officers, moved through the streets alongside local residents dressed in long gowns called *chogas*. The wealthier locals rode in covered litters known as *doolies*. The atmosphere was clamorous and festive. Everywhere one looked, there was a new exotic sight to greet the senses.

A crowd of onlookers had gathered around an emaci-

"They'll fascinate you with a knife right through your gullet, beggin' your pardon, Father," Learoyd said. "Far be it from me to tell a missionary priest his Christan duty; I've met enough men of the cloth to know they'll take the Lord's word into the jaws of Hell if that's where they see fit to go, but it's no country for a woman, Father. If I were you, I'd send Miss Cross here back to Simla, where a lady can be treated like a lady. You'd be doin' her a favor, and that's God's truth."

"In other words, Private Learoyd," Andre said, "you're saying that you do not think me fit for such a challenge?"

"No offense, miss," Learoyd said, "but the Pathan highlands are no place for one of the weaker sex."

She smiled. "Weaker, Private Learoyd?"

"I do not impute your strength of spirit, miss," said Learoyd, "I speak of physical strength. It's a hard land you plan on goin' to."

"And you are strong enough to brave the dangers, whereas I am not?" said Andre.

Learoyd grinned. "Well, I'm a man, miss. And dealin' with the Pathans is a man's work."

"Prove it," she said, setting her elbow on the table in position for an arm wrestle. "Prove I'm weaker than you, and I may reconsider my position."

Mulvaney roared and slapped the table. "Now *that's* what I call spunk!" he said. "Go on, Learoyd, me son, 'ave a go. It's as good an excuse to 'old a lady's 'and as any!"

"Surely you're joking," said Learoyd.

Andre stared at him deadpan, her hand still held ready to grasp his.

"Come now, miss, I'd be loath to hurt you," said Learoyd. "This is foolishness. I'm right sorry if I hurt your pride. I'll take it back now, right?"

"You said you were stronger than I," said Andre. "I

say you're a liar. Prove you're not."

"Now, miss," said Learoyd, clearly annoyed, "that's no way to talk. Tell her I meant no offense, Father, and we'll leave it at that."

Lucas shrugged. "Miss Cross, as I have learned, is a woman of an independent thought and unusual talents. Once she has made her mind up, she will not be dissuaded. You've made a statement you purport is true, Private. It appears you'll have to prove it or have it known you were afraid to."

"What a load of rubbish," said Learoyd. He frowned. "Right, then." He put up his elbow and grasped Andre's hand. "I'll be as gentle as I can, miss. But mind now, you insisted on this. Say when, Mulvaney."

"On three," said the burly private. "One . . . two . . . *three!*"

Learoyd's hand smacked the table before he knew what happened. His eyes grew wide. Ortheris spat tea as he tried to keep from laughing.

"That wasn't fair," said Andre. "You weren't even trying. You were going to give in a little, just to humor me. One more time, and this time for real." She put up her arm again.

"Faith, and you're a different sort of woman altogether," said Learoyd. "Very well, then. But this time I won't hold back. I give you fair warning."

"I expect no less than for you to do your best," said Andre.

"Mulvaney," said Learoyd.

"Right. One . . . two . . . *three!*"

Both exerted pressure on the signal. Learoyd's mouth dropped open as Andre's arm refused to budge. Ortheris and Mulvaney, thinking he was toying with her, started chuckling, but it became apparent to them in a moment that Learoyd wasn't fooling, that he was exerting all his strength to try and put her down and he wasn't getting anywhere. They stared at the contest in astonishment.

"Blimey!" said Mulvaney. "I must be dreamin'!"

"Come on, Learoyd!" said Ortheris. "You can't let a *woman* put you down, now can you?"

Mulvaney frowned. "Stop muckin' about, me son."

"Who's muckin' about?" said Learoyd. "She's as strong as I am!"

"Only *as* strong?" Andre said, smiling. Learoyd's arm slowly began to give.

"Well, I'll be buggered!" said Mulvaney, forgetting he was in the presence of a priest. Both he and Ortheris started to cheer Learoyd on, but it was to no avail. Learoyd gritted his teeth; Learoyd turned red with effort; Learoyd grunted; Learoyd strained, and his arm was still inexorably forced lower until at last the back of his hand touched the surface of the table.

Learoyd gasped as Andre let him go. Ortheris shook his head with amazement. "If I 'adn't seen it for myself," he said, "I'd never 'ave believed it!"

"Learoyd, that was a disgraceful exhibition, mate," Mulvaney said. "Wait'll the lads in B Comp'ny find out about this!"

"*You* have a go at her!" said Learoyd. "She's got the strength of a bloody dockworker!"

Mulvaney, of course, had to rise to the occasion, and being at least twice as strong as Learoyd, he was able to put Andre down, but not without some effort. "Well, sod me!" said Mulvaney, then realized what he had said and flushed.

"It's quite all right, Private Mulvaney," said Andre.

"Miss Cross is a most unusual and surprising woman, wouldn't you agree?" said Lucas.

Andre was rubbing her arm.

"I 'aven't done you any 'arm, 'ave I, mum?" said

Mulvaney, genuinely concerned. "Nothin' against you, y'understand, but I'm quite strong, an' you just 'ad a good match with Learoyd, 'ere."

"I'm all right," said Andre, though her arm was sore and her hand felt as if it had been squeezed in a vise.

"I take back everything I said," Learoyd said with admiration. "Tell me, miss, how did you come to be so strong? It's truly remarkable."

"I grew up on a farm," said Andre truthfully, for she did grow up on a farm in the Basque country of the Pyrenees in the 12th century. She did not mention that a large part of her strength was due to having been raised as a boy who was trained to be a squire to a knight. The not inconsiderable weight of an English broadsword did wonders for arm development.

"Well, I'll grant you this, miss," said Learoyd, "if any white woman was fit enough to travel among the Pathans, that woman is yourself. Though why anyone would want to go there is beyond me."

"Why do you go, Private Learoyd?" Andre said.

"Because I'm a Tommy, miss, and I go where I'm ordered," Learoyd said.

"That isn't the real reason," Andre said. "If the duty was unbearable to you, ways could be found to avoid it. You could request a transfer. If no other option were available, you could even take more drastic measures. As a nurse, I've seen many cases where men had avoided duty due to being accidentally wounded in some manner, and though I'm not a physician, it didn't take one to see that the wounds were self-inflicted."

Learoyd looked scandalized. "Now what sort of a man would do a thing like that, miss? That's a coward's way!"

"I see," said Andre. "Then it becomes a question of priorities. If survival were your first priority, then you would pursue any course that would ensure it. Yet if shooting yourself in the foot is something you would regard as cowardly and dishonorable, then clearly you have other priorities that take precedence over survival. Honor, for example. Displaying bravery in battle. Perhaps hand in hand with those go the desire for adventure and the thrill of undertaking a challenge. Those are not exclusively masculine attributes, Private Learoyd. If I were to turn around and go back to the capital at Simla, after having come all this way, I would be avoiding a duty, in a manner of speaking. If I were a man, you'd call that cowardly, wouldn't you?"

"I suppose I would at that, miss," said Learoyd.

"When were you and Miss Cross plannin' to depart upon your journey, Father?" said Mulvaney.

"We were hoping that we'd be able to travel with the regiment," said Lucas. "At least, most of the way, until it became necessary for us to strike out on our own."

"I can't see as where that'd be a problem," said Mulvaney. "The regiment can always use another doctor on a long march."

"In that case we'd best be on our way to the cantonment," said Delaney. "I need to report in, and the Father here needs to speak with the commanding officer."

"That would be General Sir Bindon Blood," said Learoyd. "He's the chief of staff."

"What sort of men is he?" said Delaney.

"Is this an officer asking an enlisted man his opinion of another officer?" Learoyd said, grinning.

"No," said Finn, smiling, "this is merely one soldier asking another's opinion of a mutual superior."

"Ah, I see," said Learoyd. "Well, in that case, what you think of Brigadier-General Sir Bindon Blood will depend entirely upon your personality. As far as his qualities as a soldier are concerned, they're absolutely first rate. You share a common heritage in that you're both Irish, though I daresay his clan is probably a great deal older than yours, sir. The general came out of the Indian Military College at Addiscombe, so he's more than well enough prepared for service on the frontier. He first held a commission in the Royal Engineers and came to India in '71, where he saw active service with the Jawaki Expedition. He then went to fight in the Zulu War in '79, followin' which he fought in the Afghan War. Then off to Egypt with the Highland Brigade and a right set-to at Tel-el-Kebir. Khedive's Star, medal and clasp and the third class of the Medjidie. Back in India again, he reorganized the Sappers and Miners and was appointed chief of staff to Sir Robert Low. He's put in a hard thirty-seven years of soldierin', plays a keen game of polo, and has taken game from wild pig to tiger in these parts. There's some that like him, some that don't, but you won't find any to dispute that Cap'n Blood's one damned fine soldier."

"Cap'n Blood?" said Andre. "I thought you said he was a general?"

" 'E is, mum," said Mulvaney. "We call 'im Cap'n Blood 'cause 'e's descended from the ruddy pirate o' the same name."

"And right proud 'e is of it, to boot," said Ortheris.

"If an army's to be sent to fight the bloody Pathans, then Blood's the man to lead it," Learoyd said, with a chuckle. "I don't envy you the task you've set yourself, Father. The tribes are restless, and it'll be hard preachin' to them when you're English, if it's the English they'll be fightin'."

"But it isn't I who will be fighting them," said Lucas. "I'm not a soldier, but a man of God."

"The mullahs may 'ave a thing or two to say 'bout that as well," said Ortheris. "You're forgettin', Father, you'll be more than just a rival to 'em. You'll be a rival who can give the tribes the benefit o' modern medicine, which no fakir or 'oly man can do.''

"That's true enough, Father," said Learoyd. "The mullahs will want you out. Failin' that, they'll doubtless want you dead. You'd be vastly better off settin' up shop in an army fort and havin' the sick people come to you, rather than goin' out and doin' your doctorin' and preachin' in the hills."

"But then I wouldn't know what's happening in the hills, would I?" said Lucas. "The only tribespeople who'd come to a fort would be those who were desperately ill and could make the journey. No, if a missionary is to succeed, he has to go out among the people."

"Then all I can say is good luck to you, Father," said Mulvaney. "There's strange rumblin's up in the 'ills, and you mark me words, there'll be the devil to pay before we make an end of it."

"What do you mean?" said Andre.

"You'll find out soon enough, miss," said Learoyd. "And when you do, you might well wish you'd taken my advice and gone back to Simla."

3 ═══════════════════════

General Sir Bindon Blood paced back and forth across the floor, his hands clasped behind his back, his eyes seeming to stare off into infinity as he spoke. He was a striking, robust figure of a man, dressed in khakis and highly polished riding boots. He bore himself erect and his slightest movement reflected a charismatic magnetism. Even his pacing seemed dramatic. Despite the sweat stains on his uniform blouse, he seemed to be completely unaffected by the oppressive heat. He had either grown accustomed to it or had simply decided that it wasn't going to bother him.

"As a physician, Father," he was saying, "you would certainly be most welcome to acccompany us on the march. We shall be traveling with three full brigades, and we can doubtless expect casualties, not only from hostiles, but from the rough terrain we shall have to cover. Moreover, we shall have to cover it in a hurry. Yet I would dissuade you, if I could, from your plan of leaving us to travel amongst the tribesmen. In that regard, the timing is most unfortunate.''

"How so, General?" said Lucas.

"We are in the middle of a situation which could lead to a full-scale frontier war, Father," General Blood said. "I have just received a telegram from the adjutant-general in India, appointing me to the command of the Malakand Field Force and instructing me to proceed at once to the relief of the garrison at Chakdarra. They are hard pressed, very hard pressed indeed. The army here on the frontier is continually faced with one insurrection after another. We must hold the Khyber Pass because it is the most direct route into India, and so there is ceaseless fighting in that great rift. Now, word reaches me that some new mullah, an Afridi holy man named Sayyid Akbar, is preaching jehad and recruiting thousands of tribesmen into his Ghazi army to prepare for the Night of the Long Knives. We must also hold the Malakand Pass because we need to keep the road to Chitral open. We must keep the road to Chitral open because some dunderhead decided that holding Chitral was essential to our Forward Policy. And so it goes, one dustup after another, simply because politicians look at points upon a map and make their decisions in utter ignorance of the character of the land or of its people. Meaning no disrespect, Father, but I fear you may have made the same sort of mistake. I wonder if you are fully aware of what it is you plan to undertake. I wonder if you know anything of the country.

"The land we're going to is a savage wilderness. The Himalayas are nearly four hundred miles in breadth and more than sixteen hundred in length. The westernmost ranges of these mountains, the Hindu Kush, are all that divide our Eastern empire from territory controlled by Russia. The land has been cracked by time and gouged by torrential rainfall. It has been ravaged by ice and snow and baked by a merciless sun. Rainfall has cut mammoth gutters called *nullahs* into the silt deposits of the valleys. Sometimes these are great dry cracks in the land which form gorges up to one hundred feet deep and several hundred yards wide. Often they have streams flowing through them—not the sort of streams you see in our English countryside, but devilishly cold, fast-flowing mountain rapids which, with the slightest degree of additional rainfall or snowmelt, become roaring and torrential rivers which can sweep you off your feet and dash you to pieces on jagged rocks. The mountains above the valleys are steep and rockstrewn, difficult to climb even for a seasoned alpinist.

"The inhabitants of these regions are utter savages. Tribe wars upon tribe. Khan attacks khan. Bloodfeuds are as common as trollops in Piccadilly. You take the ferocity of the Zulu, add it to the craft of the American redskin and the marksmanship of the Boer, and you have your Pathan, a violent, murderous aborigine. Every man jack of them is a soldier. Each one goes about armed to the teeth. And they dearly love to fight. We have a sizable number of them in our own forces, a mixed blessing at best, for like as not they'll desert us whenever the mood strikes them and turn the Martinis we issue them back on us. Yet we cannot afford to do without them. We require the manpower; we need their skills and knowledge of the terrain. So long as we feed them regularly and give them something of a better standard of living than they can expect to find with their own tribes, as well as provide them with a license to kill with impunity, chances are they'll remain with us and fight well for us, even against their own people. Such is the character of those you hope to convert to Christianity. They are a murderous, ignorant, and superstitious people, easily roused and well-nigh impossible to pacify.

Yet we must pacify them. That is my duty, Father. I will not attempt to instruct you in yours, but I can at least see to it that your choice is an informed one.''

"Some of your men have told me much the same thing," said Lucas. "I can well appreciate the situation, General, but it changes nothing. I, too, have my duty, as you pointed out."

Blood nodded curtly. "Well-spoken, Father. All's been said, then. See the quartermaster about drawing some supplies. We leave on a forced march first thing in the morning. And on your way out, see the clerk and leave the names of your next of kin."

"You're most kind, General," said Lucas.

Blood grunted. "Oh, and one more thing, before you leave. This is a military expedition, you understand. As such, I'm in no position to spare you any orderlies. I travel without one myself. However, seeing that you are traveling in company with a lady, may I suggest you retain one of the locals as a *khawasin*. He'll have to double as a *bhisti*, carrying water for the troops when needed, but that's expected. I would suggest you hire a Hindustani, they're generally less trouble. Now you'll excuse me, Father, I have a great many things to see to. The quartermaster will see to it that you and Miss Cross have a place to bed down for the night. Enjoy it, it'll be the last decent night's sleep you're likely to get in a long time."

After having seen to their supplies for the next day's march, Lucas and Andre went to the barracks in search of Finn. He proved easy enough to find. All they had to do was follow the sound of raucous laughter and drinkfueled song. It was Mulvaney's voice that carried the verse while the others joined in the chorus of a barrack-room ballad made popular by Kipling.

"I went into a public-'ouse to get a pint o' beer,
The publican 'e up an' sez, 'We serve no red-coats
here.'
The girls be'ind the bar they laughed an' giggled
fit to die,
I outs into the street again an' to myself sez I:
O it's Tommy this, an' Tommy that, an'
'Tommy go away';
But it's 'Thank you, Mister Atkins,' when the
band begins to play.
The band begins to play, my boys, the band
begins to play.
O it's 'Thank you, Mister Atkins,' when the
band begins to play."

Ortheris took up the next verse, howling like a stray dog.

"I went into a theatre as sober as could be,
They gave a drunk civilian room, but 'adn't none
for me;
They sent me to the gallery or round the music-
'alls,
But when it comes to fightin', Lord! they'll shove
me in the stalls!
For it's Tommy this, an' Tommy that, an'
'Tommy, wait outside';
But it's 'Special train for Atkins' when the
trooper's on the tide.
O it's 'Special train for Atkins' when the
trooper's on the tide."

Learoyd's turn came next and he sounded considerably more melodious than his cohorts.

"Yes, makin' mock o' uniforms that guard you
      while you sleep
Is cheaper than them uniforms, an' they're starva-
      tion cheap;
An' hustlin' drunken soldiers when they're goin'
      large a bit
Is five times better business than paradin' in full
      kit.
   Then it's Tommy this, an' Tommy that, an'
      'Tommy, 'ow's yer soul?'
   But it's 'Thin red line of 'eroes' when the drums
      begin to roll.
   The drums begin to roll, my boys, the drums
      begin to roll,
   O it's 'Thin red line of 'eroes' when the drums
      begin to roll."

Delaney picked up the honors for the next verse, lay-
ing into it with gusto, to the applause of the soldiers,
who were unaccustomed to having their officers being
so regular around them.

"We aren't no thin red 'eroes, nor we aren't no
      blackguards too.
But single men in barricks, most remarkable like
      you;
An' if sometimes our conduck isn't all your fancy
      paints,
Why, single men in barricks don't grow into
      plaster saints;
   While it's Tommy this, an' Tommy that, an'
      'Tommy, fall be'ind',
   But it's 'Please to walk in front, sir,' when
      there's trouble in the wind.

*There's trouble in the wind, my boys, there's
          trouble in the wind.*
*O it's 'Please to walk in front, sir,' when there's
          trouble in the wind."*

The entire group was struck dumb with amazement
when Andre chimed in with the final verse.

*"You talk 'o better food for us, an' schools, an'
          fires, an' all:*
*We'll wait for extry rations if you treat us ra-
          tional.*
*Don't mess about the cook-room slops, but prove
          it to our face*
*The Widow's Uniform is not the soldier-man's
          disgrace."*

Delaney joined in with her on the chorus, and after a
moment's disbelieving hesitation, the others did as well.

*"For it's Tommy this, an' Tommy that, an'
          'Chuck him out, the brute!'*
*But it's 'Savior of 'is country' when the guns
          begin to shoot;*
*An' it's Tommy this, an' Tommy that, an'
          anything you please,*
*An' Tommy ain't a bloomin' fool, you bet that
          Tommy sees!"*

" 'Pon my soul, miss," said Mulvaney, rising to his
feet along with the others, "that was a right proper finish to a right proper barracks song. An' it's the first
time I ever 'eard a lady sing so lustily since I was in the
good ol' East End at Miss Violet McKenzie's—"

"Tavern," Learoyd said very quickly. "She was a

lovely singer, Miss McKenzie was. Warmed our hearts to hear her sing, it did."

Mulvaney turned crimson and looked down at the floor. Ortheris pretended to have something caught in his throat.

"I'm very flattered, gentlemen," said Andre, "to be compared to someone with so much . . . warmth."

Ortheris broke into a fit of coughing.

"Do sit down, gentlemen," said Andre. "No need to stand on my account. And someone please give Private Ortheris a drink before he strangulates himself. Then someone can give me one, as well."

"So how did your conference with the general go, Father?" Delaney said.

"He attempted to induce me to change my mind," said Lucas, "but said I would be welcome to accompany the force if I was dead set on going."

"Well, then, welcome to you, Father," said Mulvaney. "An' mind now, you boys watch your lips in the presence o' the clergy an' his lady!"

"Somehow that didn't quite come out sounding right, Mulvaney," said Learoyd wryly.

"Well, bleedin' 'Ell," Mulvaney said, "you know what I damn well mean!"

Learoyd rolled his eyes.

"Perhaps you gentlemen could be of some assistance," Lucas said. "Where might I find a Hindustani attendant for myself and Miss Cross on the march?"

Before anyone could reply, a thin, bedraggled young Hindu dressed in nothing save a dhoti and a turban leaped up from where he had been crouching in a dim corner like a dog and came running up to stand bowing before Lucas.

"Father Sahib wishes *khawasin*? I am good *khawasin*! Work very hard! Very cheap! Serve very well! Take good care of Father Sahib and Memsahib!''

"Well, it seems we have a volunteer," said Lucas.

"You could do better than him, Father," said Learoyd. "He wouldn't be your best choice. He's an untouchable, you see. Outside the caste system. None of the other Hindus would have anythin' to do with him. Poor beggar wouldn't have any company on the march at all, no one to talk to."

"He could talk to us," said Andre.

"Any reason why we can't take him?" said Lucas.

"The choice is yours, Father," said Learoyd.

"Good. It's settled, then."

The Hindu dropped to his knees and began kissing Lucas's boots, intermingling English thank-yous with a torrent of Hindi.

"Come on now, up with you, Din!" said Mulvaney, hauling him to his feet. "That's no way to act before a proper Englishman! 'E's a priest, not no bleedin' rajah!''

"Well, you bought yourself a faithful hound, Father," said Learoyd. "His name is Gunga Din and he speaks English, after a fashion. Nice enough chap, though a bit childlike, like most of his sort. He followed the regiment here all the way from Simla. He's been a sort of unofficial regimental *bhisti*, but I guess he's yours now."

"Is that all he has to wear?" said Lucas.

"It's all 'e's got, period," said Mulvaney. "Not 'ardly equipped for a march to Chitral, 'e ain't."

"Well, we shall have to do something about that," said Lucas. "We'll have to send him to the quartermaster to get properly equipped and to get some decent clothing."

Din's face lit up. "Uniform, Father Sahib? Din be good soldier with uniform!"

"Soldier?" said Mulvaney, while Din shrank back from him.

"Why not?" said Lucas.

"Why not, indeed?" said Ortheris. "Just send 'im over to the quartermaster and tell 'im to ask for a full kit and a suit of khakis. The quartermaster, kind soul that 'e is, will comply without a moment's 'esitation." The men laughed.

Din's face took on a crestfallen expression as he saw his hopes of obtaining a khaki uniform fade as quickly as they had arisen.

"Well, now, surely if the quartermaster knew it was for me," said Lucas, "he'd do it. After all, we can't very well have Miss Cross being attended by a half-naked man."

"Right," Delaney said. "Ortheris, since you pointed out the problem, perhaps you'd be so good as to accompany Din to see the quartermaster?"

"Per'aps I will," said Ortheris, "after I've done with this whiskey."

"Now, Ortheris," said Delaney.

Ortheris scowled. "I knew it was too good to last," he said. "Sooner or later an officer's bound to start actin' like an officer. Come on then, Din. We'll go an' get you your soldier suit."

He left with the joyful Gunga Din in tow. Learoyd smiled. "I'd say you made yourself a friend for life there, Father."

"From what I hear about where we're going, I'd say I could use all the friends I can get," said Lucas. "Tell me, Private Mulvaney—"

"Just plain ol' Mulvaney, Father. Everyone calls me that."

"All right, Mulvaney. What can you tell me about what's happening at Chakdarra?"

"Bloody fair mess is what's 'appenin', if you ask me. Some damn fool sod in Simla, sittin' on his bleedin'—"

"Mulvaney!" said Learoyd. "Perhaps it would be better if *I* were to explain. Mind you now, Father, I'm not privy to what's told to the command staff, but scuttlebutt is generally pretty reliable in this outfit. Chitral is some hundred fifty miles north of here and about four miles or so straight up. Now, because it looks so nice and well situated on a map, someone went and decided that the Sirkar ought to take an interest in it, as it were, and so a political agent was ensconced there. 'Round about five years ago or so, the local high muckamuck there, a sort of king called the Mehtar of Chitral, Aman-ul-Mulk, by name, up and died. The problem was, Aman left about a score of sons and not much in the way of a proper line of succession. Several of them killed each other off while tryin' to take the throne, and it looked as though things would eventually even out all by themselves, until Umra Khan stepped into the picture."

"Who's Umra Khan?" said Andre.

"A bloody Pathan warlord," said Mulvaney.

"The Khan of Jandul," Learoyd said. "Also known amongst us all by several somewhat less exalted appellations. Actually, the whole thing was more or less our fault, in a way. If we'd kept ourselves well out of it, our boys wouldn't now be in such a stew up there. Unfortunately the Forward Policy has its own curious sort of momentum. Aman was always friendly to the Sirkar, and Simla had no trouble with him. In return for arms and ammunition, as well as six thousand rupees a year, he became our ally. We posted an agent to Gilgit and that was that. Then Aman decided that he wanted more, so the annual payment was doubled. There was no further trouble till Aman died. One of his sons, Afzal, happened to be in a position to seize the reins of power. He immediately started killing off his brothers, but the litter was quite sizable. He couldn't get them all at once.

"Anyway," Learoyd continued, "Afzal claimed the title of Mehtar and asked for recognition from Simla. The bloody fools gave it to him, figurin', I suppose, to be Johnny-on-the-spot with the new man. Never mind he murdered several of his brothers and had the rest seeking sanctuary with the neighboring chiefs. Now the eldest brother, Nizam, appealed to Simla for help. Of course, our people could hardly give it to him, having already recognized his little brother. Shortly thereafter, Afzul, not to be confused with Afzal, returned to Chitral. This was Sher Afzul, the new Mehtar's uncle. He promptly killed his nephew Afzal as well as yet another brother in the bargain. Exit Afzal, the late Mehtar, enter Afzul, the new Mehtar. Bit of a Chinese fire drill, but it grows more absurd. Having recognized the late Mehtar, it appeared bad form for the boys at Simla to recognize his murderer, so they gave Nizam 250 Cashmere rifles, which in turn encouraged a sizable number of the local tribesmen to join up as well. Nizam marches on his uncle, who sends over a thousand men to stop him. Said thousand men immediately desert to Nizam's side. Uncle Mehtar, fearful for his life, and rightfully so, performs a rather graceless abdication and beats a hasty retreat.

"You follow all this so far?" Learoyd said, smirking. "We now have Mehtar Number Three, good ol' Nizam the Nephew. He, however, proves so inept at Mehtarin' that in order to help keep the peace, it's decided to send Captain Younghusband and a full battalion to reinforce the garrison at Gilgit. Ready trumpet fanfare . . . enter Umra Khan, the aforementioned Pathan warlord. Turns out that yet another son-of-Aman—or son of something else not a man at all, if you get my meanin'—young chap named Amir, had taken refuge with the Khan of Jandul. Said son appears in Chitral, properly respectful of his brother the Mehtar, and claims to have escaped from Umra Khan, who had not used him kindly. Since brother Amir appears so properly respectful, brother Nizam the Mehtar makes him welcome, upon which Amir murders Nizam in a properly respectful manner. Where are we now, Mehtar Number Four or thereabouts? No matter, we're still keepin' it all in the family.

"Now the agent and the soldiers in Chitral have no idea what to do. Recognize yet another new Mehtar? Might be too hasty. After all, there're still a few other sons runnin' about here and there, no tellin' the rate of turnover in this job. So word goes out to Simla—would someone mind very much tellin' us what to do about this situation, if it wouldn't be too much trouble?

"Meanwhile, Umra Khan the Aforementioned, who, as it turned out, hadn't used Amir badly at all—Amir's the current aspirant to longevity at Mehtarin', you'll recall—said Umra Khan begins to march with a large force upon Chitral. Just to lend a hand, you understand. Amir, in his new precarious position, is somewhat leery of said hand and so he sends out a force to meet the khan's. The khan prevails after a bit of a dustup, exit Amir. Now Umra Khan, havin' no great desire to Mehtar himself, invites Sher Afzul—that's the uncle who was Number Two Mehtar—or was it Number Three? No matter. Anyway, Number Two now becomes Number Four. Or is it Five? Whatever. And just in case we didn't like it, Umra Khan and Sher Afzul announce that they will fight if we oppose them. Now one knows that isn't the sort of thing one says to an Englishman, much less a garrison full of Englishmen who are already confused about this comedy of errors. So of course the garrison opposed them, with the result being that the

14th Sikhs were massacred and their officers taken prisoner. Fort Chitral, miles away from nowhere, finds itself beseiged.

"Outnumbered by fifty to one, Surgeon-Major Robertson finds himself havin' to defend the fort with about three hundred rounds per man and not much in the way of supplies. One massed attack follows another. The fort is fired on repeatedly, yet somehow Robertson holds on and keeps the fort from burnin' to the ground. He holds on long enough for Sir Robert Low to arrive with three brigades and Colonel Kelly with one. Both commanders had to fight for every inch of ground along the way. They save Robertson, put Umra Khan to flight, and breathe a mighty sigh of relief, thinkin' its all over. And just to be on the safe side, so they don't have to fight for every inch of ground goin' back, it's decided to establilsh a garrison in the Malakand Pass to keep the road open. Now we come at last to a gentlemen who calls himself Sadullah, referred to hereabouts as the Mad Mullah. Rather like that Mahdi chap General 'Chinese' Gordon ran afoul of in Khartoum. Am I losin' you?"

"No, go on," said Andre. "This is fascinating."

Learoyd grinned. "You'll find it less so, miss, I promise you. While all this was goin' on, our supposed ally in Kabul, the Emir Abdur Rahman, called a sort of council of the local holy men in all these parts, to study the Koran or some such. While he's being a genial chap to all the lads in Simla, the emir tells all the holy men about how General Gordon got his head up on a pike down in Khartoum and how we're havin' other minor troubles here and there, and he tells them that the Prophet has decreed the time has come for the infidel *firinghi*, and so on and so forth. Thus, havin' attended Sunday school, the holy men go forth to spread the word. And our friend Sadullah spreads it finer than any man I know. Next thing the boys up in the Malakand know, they've got themselves a bloody jehad upon their heads.

"Accordin' to the latest communication, they were havin' themselves a go at a few chukkers of polo when about 10,000 Ghazis came screamin' down their throats. They're hangin' on up there, holdin' off against a hundred to one odds, and praying' like Hell, if you'll excuse the expression, Father, that we'll get there in time to save them all from bein' butchered. The Guides have already left, the lancers leave tonight, and us Tommys, bein' the least mobile, leave first thing in the mornin'."

He turned to Delaney. "You'll be good enough to clear the way for us, I'm sure, sir. We'll do what we can on our part. After all, we'll have the Father with us. You watch, he'll get there and convert them all to Christianity and they'll throw down all their weapons and join us in a chorus of 'Bringin' in the Sheaves.' "

"An' I couldn't 'ave told it better meself," Mulvaney said, " 'ceptin' I wouldn't 'ave taken so bloody long a time about it." He pushed back his chair and got up from the table. "Gentlemen, and lady, you'll excuse me, I am sure, but I've to to go an' see about me kit." He tossed Delaney a half drunken salute and shambled off.

"Take my advice, Father," said Learoyd. "Go home."

"I'm afraid I cannot, Private Learoyd," said Lucas.

Learoyd rose. "Well, then, much as it may go against your Christian conscience, you may find it more useful to lay aside your Bible for a time and do your convertin' with a rifle. Good night to you."

Lucas looked across the table at Finn and Andre, his mouth set in a grim expression. "Who was the idiot who decided this would be a good scenario for temporal confrontations?''

Andre shook her head. "I didn't hear anything in what he said that contradicted history. If there are any anomalies present, if there's any interference, it hasn't affected the scenario yet.''

"That we know of," said Finn. "I'd keep an eye on Learoyd if I were you, Lucas. Despite the occasional lapse into slang, it strikes me that his conversation is way too educated for a mere army private. And scuttlebut or no, he's a lot more well informed than the average soldier.''

"That had occurred to me," said Lucas. "I think I'll stick close to all three of them.''

Outside, a bugle sounded, and Finn stood up. "That's first call for assembly," he said. "My unit's getting ready to move out.''

Andre reached out and took his arm. "Be careful, Finn.''

"I will.''

"Don't take any chances out there," Lucas said. "If it starts to look bad, use your warp disc and get the hell out. If we don't rendezvous at Chakdarra, we'll meet here, at that same shop in the bazaar.''

"Right," said Finn.

"Good luck.''

"You too. Stay close to Blood, if you can. He seems to be the most important figure in this scenario.''

"Got it.''

Assembly blew.

"Got to go," said Finn. "I'll meet you in Chakdarra.''

Outside, there were the sounds of horses and pack animals massing as the 11th Bengal Lancers prepared to ride out to the relief of Chakdarra.

"I wish we were going with him," Andre said.

"So do I," said Lucas, "but this improves our chances. If anything gets out of whack up ahead, Finn can scout the situation and clock back to let us know. Besides, he's right. We've got to protect the important figures in this scenario. And Blood's the most important one on hand right now."

The door burst open with a slam. Standing in the entrance was a dashing young blond officer in the uniform of a subaltern in the 4th Hussars. He saw Lucas and Andre and politely removed his shako.

"Excuse me, Father, madam. I wonder if you could tell me where I might find General Sir Bindon Blood? I've just arrived to join the march. My name is Winston Churchill."

4 _____

Sharif Khan was a self-made man. He began his khanate by the simple expedient of stealing a rifle from one of the British pickets at Landi Kotal. In the dead of night, while the picket slept, he had crept up to him and stolen his breech-loading Martini-Henry, as well as several belts of ammunition. This made him a man to be reckoned with in the small Afridi village where he had settled. With the rifle to back up his new important status, he prevailed upon several of the young men in the village to build a gun tower as an addition to his small brick house, and he instructed them in the proper way of loopholing the walls to provide embrasures, as well as in constructing a high, surrounding wall around the entire dwelling. Thus ensconced in this miniature fort with its gun tower overlooking all the village, he proclaimed himself a khan.

Within a short time of arriving in the village, he had led its people in an attack upon a neighboring settlement. In this manner he quickly increased his domain,

making feudal vassals of those he subjugated. Within a
short time he had gained a reputation in the region as a
chief to be feared and respected. He lived in a bigger
house now, a small fort that was opulently furnished, as
befitted the status of a khan. He had well-trained
bodyguards and he obtained more money through his
raids, which he used to purchase more rifles, ammunition, and supplies. He had acquired a harem, small, but
of extremely high quality. And now he waited to be noticed.

Sharif Khan was not his real name. He was last
known as Reese Hunter, a captain in the First Division
of the Temporal Corps. Yet that was not his real name
either. The real Reese Hunter had died in 17th century
France, his throat slit by an assassin. Sharif Khan had
been known by many names. One of them was Barry
Martingale, once a sergeant in the Temporal Corps.
Barry Martingale had been a cover identity, carefully
constructed to allow an agent of Temporal Intelligence
to infiltrate a terrorist organization headed by a man
named Drakov. The man who had been Barry Martingale, then Reese Hunter, and who was now the Afridi
chieftain, Sharif Khan, was a TIA agent known by the
codename Phoenix.

The TIA's senior field agent before Phoenix had been
murdered by an assassin who had insinuated herself into
his private life. It was a mistake Phoenix would never
make. He trusted no one except one man—the enig-
matic Dr. Darkness, the man who was faster than light.

Manifesting from the tachyon state that allowed him
to cross the boundries of space and time in a near-zero
interval, Darkness appeared in Sharif Khan's bedroom
like a ghost materializing from the ether. Dressed in a
long black Inverness and a wide-brimmed black slouch
hat, he looked incongruous in his surroundings. His ap-

pearance was a marked contrast to that of Phoenix, who wore baggy white linen trousers buttoned at the ankles, curl-toed boots, a wide blue sash, and an embroidered vest over a loose white shirt. Cosmetic surgery had darkened the pigmentation of the agent's skin, and his normally blond hair was now jet black and worn down to his shoulders. His blue turban was fastened by a golden clasp. He smiled and gave Darkness the traditional Islamic greeting of a slight bow and genuflection with the open hand.

The gaunt, lugubrious features of the scientist seemed to blur for an instant before they resolved themselves into a grimace of distaste. He gestured with his blackthorn walking stick, indicating their surroundings.

"This place looks like a Persian whorehouse. And what is that hideous smell?"

"It's dinner, I'm afraid," said Phoenix. "It smells like goat meat boiled in Cosmoline, but it doesn't taste too bad once you get used to it." He smiled. "I'd have them set another place, but my wives might become upset if you suddenly appeared out of thin air at the dinner table."

"Yes, I believe I saw two of your wives leaving this room before I manifested," Darkness said. "They looked all of fourteen."

Phoenix shrugged. "In their prime and eminently marriageable by Afridi standards. I could hardly have allowed the most desirable young women in this village to marry someone else. Sharif Khan has to maintain a certain image."

"I'll refrain from commenting on the nature of that image," Darkness said wryly. "Did you have much trouble disposing of your identity as Barry Martingale?"

"Some," said Phoenix. "The commandos compli-

cated matters by giving me a new identity. I would have
died of plasma burns if they hadn't clocked me to that
army hospital. They bought my cover and believed I was
a deserter. They didn't want me to be arrested, so they
altered official records, believe it or not, and gave me
the identity of an MIA. They thought they were helping
me when they switched the data in Martingale's jacket
with Reese Hunter's. Instead they created an official file
through which I could be traced if I ever slipped up. I
had to make sure Hunter was accounted for somehow."

"So what became of your identity as Hunter?" Darkness said.

"He checked out of the hospital and requested a brief
reorientation leave." Phoenix grinned. "After all, he'd
been out of action for a while. I managed to stage a con-
venient accident. Captain Hunter died in a skimmer
crash in San Diego. No trace of the body after the explosion. That way, no one asks any questions, and both
Martingale and Hunter are disposed of. After that it
was a simple matter to wrangle this assignment. The
Referees have given over jurisdiction in this matter to
the army, which made it the First Division's mission.
You can imagine how Temporal Intelligence took that.
They can't infringe upon an adjustment mission assigned by Vargas himself, but they could send a covert
team back to gather information. I was the logical
person to head up that team."

"How many agents have you brought with you?"
Darkness said.

"Five. Two in my bodyguard and three posing as my
senior lieutenants. I picked the men myself. I think
that's enough to handle the situation if it becomes really
serious."

"It's more serious than you know," said Darkness.
"My instruments have detected massive fluctuations in

the timestream. I've been attempting to pinpoint the source, but it's impossible. The effect is not a static one. The entire timestream is rippling. It's Mensinger's worst nightmare come true."

"Jesus," Phoenix said. "Are you sure?"

"Of course I'm sure," said Darkness. "I'm not in the habit of making theoretical pronouncements. Not even Vargas suspects how serious it is, and he has a doctorate in Zen physics. He believes it can be resolved by a temporal adjustment. He doesn't understand that it's gone beyond that. I think he's afraid to admit it to himself. He's been a bureaucrat too long. The truth is staring him right in the face, but he doesn't want to see it."

"Just what is the truth, exactly?" said Phoenix.

"Exactly? I don't know," said Darkness. "An alternate universe exists in a timeline parallel to ours. Perhaps it came about as a result of a massive disruption which overcame the inertia of the timeflow. Perhaps it always existed. Any number of alternate universes can exist, completely independent of each other. Something has happened that has caused two separate timelines to be brought into very close proximity. That would account for the rippling effect, the inertia of one timeline acting upon the inertia of the other, like opposing magnetic fields. Under such circumstances it would be possible for people in one timeline to travel to the other, if they could pinpoint the focus of the disruption that brought the phenomenon about. Even if they couldn't, it could still be possible, although whether or not they could do so with any degree of control, I cannot say. I, for one, am not about to attempt the experiment until I have more information. You see before you the result of what happened the last time I tried something like that. You have no idea how maddening it can be, being able to travel anywhere I please, teleporting to any point in

time and space, yet not being able to walk so much as
one step once I get there. I failed to anticipate the
influence of the Law of Baryon Conservation, and the
result was a permanent alteration of my subatomic
structure. Before I make any reconnaissance of a parallel universe, I wish to be certain of the variables. And
that's where you come in."

"I'm not sure I like the sound of that," said Phoenix.

"Relax, I won't be asking you to do anything so
esoteric as teleporting to another timeline. I need you to
pinpoint a confluence for me."

"A confluence? What's that?"

"A point at which two timelines intersect," said
Darkness. "There are two possibilities inherent in this
situation. One is that agents from the parallel timeline
have been able to identify the focus of the original
disruption and can travel to this timeline by clocking
directly to that point. However, given the rippling effect, I believe the second possibility is more likely—that
there exist a number of points of confluence where the
two timelines intersect as a result of an imbalance in the
flow of temporal inertia. One of those points is
undoubtedly located in this time period, somewhere
nearby. I want you to find it."

"How?" said Phoenix. "I mean, how the hell would
I recognize a point of confluence, or whatever the hell it
is?"

"Good question," said Darkness. "Since such a
phenomenon has never previously existed, I obviously
haven't seen one. In fact, I doubt it would something
one *could* see."

"How the hell am I supposed to find it then?" said
Phoenix.

"You expect me to tell you everything?" said
Darkness. "You're an intelligence agent. Go out and

gather some intelligence. And try displaying some on occasion. Use your initiative. The next time I see you, I'll expect some results. Good day."

Darkness tached, translating into tachyons that departed at six hundred times the speed of light. Phoenix took a deep breath and expelled it slowly.

"How the hell do you find something you can't see?" he said to himself. "And how do you find it without stumbling into it?" He looked around nervously. "I'm liable to turn a corner and wind up in another universe. That ought to be good for a few laughs."

"Your Holiness," cried the tribesman, out of breath from having run all the way from his observation post, "lancers approach!"

The man named Sadullah, known to the British as the Mad Mullah, slowly raised his head to stare at the Ghazi sentry. His deeply sunken eyes were dark and their gaze was indeed mad. They never seemed to blink. His dark skin was etched with lines of age and his hair was long, almost to his waist, and utterly white. His head was bare, as were his feet. He wore a long white robe and many amulets and charms around his neck. He sat cross-legged on a rug inside his tent, which was filled with the fumes of bhang. His eyes glittered.

"How many?" he said, his voice soft and low.

"Three, perhaps four squadrons, Your Holiness," said the sentry. "You have but to give the word and we shall sweep down upon the infidel *firinghi* and destroy them before they can arrive at the Malakand fort!"

"No," said Sadullah.

The sentry was taken aback. "But Your Holiness, if we do not attack now, they shall surely reach the Malakand fort! Then they can join forces with the *firinghi* soldiers there and march to relieve Chakdarra!"

"I want them to reach the Malakand fort," Sadullah said.

"But . . . *why*, Your Holiness?"

"Do you question me?" Sadullah said, his voice deadly.

The sentry dropped down on all fours. "No, Your Holiness! You speak with the voice of the Prophet! It is not for one so humble as I to question your methods. I only seek understanding."

"It is well," Sadullah said. "All men should seek to understand, though few succeed. Understand this, then. When the time is ripe, I shall destroy the British. I will not require the help of followers such as yourself. You may all do as you please. Your faith shall be judged in Paradise. Come the Night of the Long Knives, I shall call forth and the heavens shall open. A great host shall descend and slaughter the infidel to the last man, woman, and child. They shall be driven from our land and their blood shall nourish the soil. Those who join with me in that great, final battle shall win their way to Paradise. They shall be invulnerable. With one wave of my hand the bullets of the British will turn to water. With another their shells shall disperse upon the wind. Only those who lack true faith will be struck down. The pure of heart shall be immune to death. Thus it is written, thus it shall be.

"In the meantime, let the lancers pass. Let them ride on to the fort at Malakand, and with them, the foot soldiers who will surely follow." Sadullah slowly raised his hands and cupped them. "The Malakand is a great cup. At its bottom, there lie the infidel *firinghi*. At its rim, all around upon the cliffs, are we. Let the soldiers go into the cup, together with those who are already trapped there. When they are all together in one place," he slowly raised his hands to his mouth, "we shall take this cup . . . and drink."

• • •

"I do not understand," said Winston Churchill. "We have made almost our entire journey unimpeded. Where are the *mujahidin* of the jehad? Why have they not tried to stop us?"

"They'll be up there in them bloomin' rocks, sir," said Mulvaney, "starin' down at us an' smirkin' up their sleeves."

"Smirking?" Churchill said. "I fail to see what there would be to smirk about, Private. Sixty-eight hundred bayonets, seven hundred sabres, and twenty-four guns would hardly seem a smirking matter."

"Beggin' your pardon, sir," Mulvaney said, "an' if you don't mind me speakin' frankly, not meanin' to sound insubordinate—which ain't 'ardly on me mind —but I'd say your green was showin'."

Churchill frowned. "My *green*? Explain yourself, man."

"Well, you'e a mite young, me son—sir, I mean," Mulvaney said. "It's all very fine to get yourself a transfer from the 4th 'Ussars so you can write up this 'ere campaign for the London *Daily Telegraph*—nice way to get a bit o' action an' pick up an extra quid or two, if I say so myself—but there's a world o' difference between writin' dispatches and anticipatin' Pathans, sir. For the one you need a bit o' learnin', which you seem to 'ave done plenty of, sir. For the other you need experience, which you ain't 'ardly old enough to 'ave received very much of. Now me mates and I 'ave been out 'ere for so long our skin's startin' to turn brown, an' we've learned a thing or two about your Pathan fightin' man. 'E ain't no fool, that's what, sir."

"Meaning exactly what, Private Mulvaney?" Churchill said.

"Meanin', sir, that 'e's got a bloody good reason for not 'avin attacked us by now," Mulvaney said.

"There's been plenty o' opportunity for 'im, but 'e ain't done it, so why's that, I ask meself? Because 'e's got 'imself a better opportunity ahead, and like as not we're walkin' right into it."

"But we're almost at the Malakand fort," said Churchill. "It would seem to me that our strength has intimidated him, otherwise he would have attacked before we could have an opportunity to join forces with the troops at the garrison."

"Or 'e's waitin' to knock off two birds with one stone, sir," said Mulvaney.

"I'm afraid Mulvaney's got a point, sir," said Learoyd. "Put yourself in the Mad Mullah's place. You've got some of your men pressing the Chakdarra garrison, others harryin' the fort at Malakand. Here comes a large relief force on its way, and in order to attack them, you've got to split your own troops further to take them on. The Malakand is situated in a large depression, sort of a valley ringed by cliffs. If you can command the heights, why not wait until the relief has arrived and then ring them 'round, cuttin' them and the garrison off from Chakdarra?"

"Rubbish, man," said Churchill. "I've seen the map of the area. In order to command the heights around the Malakand, it would require a very large force indeed. Thousands, I should say."

"Now you're catchin' on, sir," said Mulvaney. "You can be sure you'll 'ave yourself a bloody entertainin' dispatch to write before too long."

The terrain they were covering was rough, extremely difficult for a large detachment with pack animals and guns. They had made good time, but making good time in the Hindu Kush range still meant going slow. Nevertheless they were within sight of the garrison at Malakand before too long, and throughout the entire journey they had encountered no resistance whatsoever, not even so much as one stray shot, which was unusual in the extreme.

Lucas and Andre traveled at the middle of the column, slightly behind Churchill. They rode on horseback, moving along at a slow walk since they were traveling with mostly infantry. Din, their Hindustani attendant, was just behind them, proudly leading their pack mule and keeping so ramrod straight a posture in his brand new khakis that it looked as though his back would break. He had managed to obtain a battered bugle somewhere, which he carried proudly and clutched to himself protectively whenever anyone came near.

"Something's wrong," said Lucas in a low voice, so that only Andre could hear him.

"I know," she said. "You've been preoccupied throughout the entire journey. It's this Churchill fellow, isn't it? You keep staring at him."

"This Churchill fellow?" Lucas said.

"Yes. What's so special about him?"

"Good Christ, you really don't know."

"Should I?"

"Well, actually, you'd be about the only one I could think of in the service who'd have a good excuse. He's not a part of your history. You went straight from the 12th century to the 27th. That leaves one hell of a big gap, though you still ought to know about him. I find that puzzling."

She frowned. "So do I. I thought my implant education was complete. If he was—is—an important historical figure, even if I didn't remember anything about him consciously, the subknowledge of the programming should have triggered my awareness of him the moment I heard his name. And there was nothing in the mission programming about him either.''

"I know. *That's* what's wrong. There's simply no way for that to be possible. Or at least there shouldn't be. That young subaltern riding up ahead grew up to be one of the most important men of the 20th century. One of the greatest political figures of his time. He became prime minister of Great Britain and led that nation through the Second World War.''

"My God,'' said Andre. "And the programmers missed *that*? How could they?''

Lucas shook his head. "They couldn't. I just can't see it. Even if someone was somehow negligent, the data banks have built in failsafes for vital information. It's been driving me crazy. And you put your finger on it. The subknowledge. I *knew* something was missing, but I couldn't figure out what it was until you said that. I knew about Churchill, but I couldn't figure out why there was a gap. Why did I know about Churchill, but didn't know about him being on this campaign? Because I didn't know it through the subknowledge of *my* implant education either! I remembered. I just plain remembered about him on my own, because I like to read history. But it's been a while since I've read any British history, or any 20th century history for that matter. I didn't remember completely. It just goes to show you how dependent we are on our subknowledge. And that's the common denominator. There was nothing about Churchill in our mission programming, and neither of us could extract anything about him from our programmed subknowledge because it simply wasn't there. And *that's* impossible.''

"You're right,'' she said. "It doesn't make sense. It should have been there.''

"You still don't understand,'' he said. "It can't *not* have been there! I can only think of one possible explanation. A temporal disruption. There isn't any record of Churchill in our subknowledge or in our supplementary mission programming because there *was* no record of a Winston Churchill as a pivotal figure in history."

"But that doesn't make sense either," Andre said. "If that's the case and a disruption occurred that has prevented—or will prevent—Churchill from following his historical template as we know . . . as *you* know it, then how could you know about it in the first place?"

Lucas stared at her. "You want to run that by me again?

"I'm not even sure what I just said." She shook her head. "What I mean is, if there isn't any historical record of Churchill, then how could you remember reading about him in your history books?"

"I see what you mean," he said. "It has to be an anomaly of Zen physics. Whatever happened that caused Churchill to be wiped from history must have happened *after* I read about him."

"I'm confused," said Andre. "How could something have happened during his lifetime and yet have taken place after you read about him in the 27th century?"

"You're confused because you never studied Zen physics," Lucas said. "I only have a well-versed layman's knowledge of it. Delaney's the only one I know who's taken the full course, and he said it almost gave him a nervous breakdown. I take that back. Our friend Dr. Darkness understands it. Hell, he could probably teach the course in his sleep. I wish to hell there was some way of getting in touch with him so we could ask him about this. Let me try to follow it through with you. Assume that some action originating in our time, in the 27th century, kicked off a chain of events that led to the disruption. For the sake of argument, let's set up a simple hypothesis. Say somebody clocked out to Minus Time, to this scenario, on the day before we went in for our mission programming. And let's say that someone killed Churchill.''

"You'd have a paradoxical situation which would have to be resolved by a disruption," Andre said.

"Right. Up until that someone clocked out to the past in order to cause the disruption, that is, killing Churchill, there was no disruption and Churchill was part of our history. If we assume that the disruption wasn't massive enough to overcome temporal inertia —and frankly, I don't see how Churchill's death wouldn't qualify as a disruption massive enough to cause a timestream split—then temporal inertia wouldn't be overcome. It would simply be affected significantly. You remember the analogy Delaney used, the timestream seen as a river? The river has a current, and that current is temporal inertia. An act that's insignificant, that is, not historically disruptive enough to affect the timeflow, is like tossing a small pebble into the river. The current or the inertia overcomes any possible effect. You wouldn't see any ripples from where you tossed the pebble in. Next, take a large rock and toss it in. The rock has mass sufficient enough to affect the current, if only temporarily. You'll see the splash, perhaps a very brief rippling effect, and then the force of the current eliminates it or compensates for it. Now take a huge, behemoth boulder—something the size of one of these damn mountains—and toss it in the river. The effect of the current is overcome. It either dams up the river somehow, or more likely, splits the flow—creating a timestream split. The river comes back together again on the other side and you have both effects working one against the other. A historical timeline in which Churchill died and one in which he didn't. *Nobody* knows how the hell that would resolve itself. It would either create a parallel universe or screw up the future six ways from Sunday. Trying to work out the possibilities has driven more than one scientist right off the deep end. Whatever it is that's happened back here—or, from where we stand now, is *about* to happen—has affected the timestream to the point that we have no historical knowledge of Churchill. It wasn't in the mission programming because the programming session took place after whatever event it was that originated in our time affected history in this time."

Andre shook her head. "That doesn't work," she said.

Lucas frowned. "Why not?"

"Granted," Andre said, "the information could be missing from my subknowledge because my implant education took place fairly recently, relatively speaking. But when did you get *your* implant education?"

"Why . . . when I enlisted, of course. But I still don't see what that has . . ." His voice trailed off.

"Uh-huh," said Andre. "When did you take up reading history as a hobby?"

"Not until well *after* I enlisted," Lucas said. "Damn! I shouldn't remember anything about Churchill either. *But why do I?*"

"I'd say we've got ourselves a real problem," Andre said.

"To which no solution can possibly exist," said Lucas, "because the problem can't exist. Only it does."

"Maybe Finn will have an answer," she said hopefully.

"Which brings up another question," Lucas said. "Will *Finn* remember anything about Winston Churchill?"

"What are you getting at?" said Andre.

"Suppose he doesn't?" Lucas said.

"Okay, so suppose that. What of it?"

"If Finn doesn't have any subknowledge of Churchill, then the whole explanation works, except in that case, *I'll* be the anomaly."

"I still don't see your point."

"Remember our hypothesis. What if something I'm about to do—or something I've already done—is the cause of the disruption?" He bit his lower lip. "Jesus, what if *I'm* the guy who's going to kill Churchill?"

5 _____

Their arrival at the Malakand was like an entrance through the doors of Hell. The troops of the garrison were worn out from fighting. Many were wounded. Many had been killed. The broken ground was littered everywhere with bodies, far too numerous for the burial details to dispose of, even if they'd had the time. The lizards and the carrion birds were feasting.

The fort itself was situated on a hill overlooking the depression known as The Crater. The position of the garrison had been spread out when the attack commenced on the twenty-sixth of July. Malakand Post, the fort itself, was in a virtually impregnable spot, but its surroundings were its weak point. To the north-northeast of the fort was The Crater, where the largest concentration of buildings stood. There was the bazaar, which now stood ruined and blackened from flames; the commissariat; the brigade offices and the mess, on a rise overlooking the depression; and an area known as Gretna Green, site of the quarters of the 45th Sikhs. To the north of the depression was a giant rock formation known as Gibraltar Tower, which was in the hands of the enemy tribesmen, who possessed superior firing position from its heights. West of the depression was a water-filled nullah. Across the nullah, through the rocks and to the north-northwest, was North Camp. The camel and transport lines were there, as well as Camp Malakand, the site of Number 8 Mountain Battery, the 31st Punjab Infantry, and a large detachment of the 11th Bengal Lancers. Back across the nullah, to the southwest of the fort, was the 24th Punjab infantry. Communications between North Camp and the Malakand Post were by telegraph. Two roads, separated by rock formations, ran parallel east of the fort to Dargai—the graded road, and the older Buddhist Road.

The officers of the fort had just returned from their game of polo when the garrison at Chakdarra telegraphed that they were under attack by a large force of Pathans. A moment later the wire was cut. The officers were still in their polo kit when the attack came.

A handful of men under the command of Lieutenant-Colonel McRae of the 45th Sikhs immediately ran to hold off the enemy's advance down the Buddhist Road until the camp could mobilize and reinforce them. They held a position at a point where the road took a sharp curve through a narrow pass. There they reenacted the stand of the Three Hundred Spartans. McRae's men kept up a steady stream of fire at an even more steady and seemingly unceasing stream of Ghazis, buying the garrison valuable time in which to organize. McRae was wounded, but he held on until nightfall. The enemy pulled back.

At the fort General Meiklejohn could see the glow of star shells from North Camp, which told him that an attack was under way there as well. More tribesmen were pressing in along the graded road, and the 24th was hotly engaged. Tribesmen commanded the heights of the Gibraltar Tower and kept up a constant sniping at the troops below while the infantry attempted to beat back the rushing advance of hundreds of fanatical swordsmen. Meiklejohn rushed from the fort, and at great peril to his life, kept moving from point to point to direct the defensive actions.

Wild fighting took place in the bazaar, a struggle of sword against bayonet as the tribesmen poured through, driving the soldiers back and capturing a large part of the ammunition reserves. Attacks continued along the high ground of the Buddhist Road and from the rocks all around. Regular fire from the rim of the depression resulted in heavy losses.

North Camp was evacuated at the first opportunity and a cavalry detachment sent to reinforce Chakdarra. Miraculously, they got through by crisscrossing the nullah while under heavy fire. Lack of proper transport caused the officers and men of North Camp to leave almost all of their possessions behind. That night the glow of flames from the north gave testimony to the looting and destruction that commenced as soon as they had left.

Continued massed attacks made it impossible for the pickets to hold their lines. They were forced to pull back to the fort, there to strengthen their defenses as much as possible by leveling the bazaar and many of the outlying buildings to cut down on the enemy's opportunities for concealment. Open lines of fire were exposed and bonfires built to illuminate the enemy's approach at night.

There was little respite. By the time the detachment of lancers Delaney rode with had arrived, the Malakand garrison had sustained heavy casualties. Three British officers were killed, ten severely wounded. Seven native officers had died, amounting to a total of twenty senior officers killed. The total losses of officers, both British and native, as well as non-commissioned officers and enlisted men, stood at 153 killed and wounded.

All around upon the hills, Delaney could see the white dots that were the white-robed Ghazis moving about. There were dozens upon dozens of tribal banners, as well as the black flags of the jehad. As night came, the cliffs all around them glowed with the light of several hundred campfires.

"Hell of a sight, eh?"

Finn turned toward the voice.

"Surgeon-Lieutenant Hugo," said the doctor.

"Lieutenant Delaney," said Finn. He held out his hand. Hugo took it in an awkward grip with his left hand. His right arm hung straight at his side, looking stiff. "You were hit?" said Finn.

Hugo gave a slight snort. "No, fortunately. Bit of temporary paralysis. Cramped, you know."

"From what?"

"Oh, Lieutenant Ford was wounded in the shoulder. Bullet cut the artery. We were under heavy fire and he was lying out in the open, so there was no opportunity to give the poor chap proper aid, don't you know. He had fainted from loss of blood. I had no other choice but to pinch the vessel shut between my thumb and forefinger. Crouched there that way for three hours until I could move him to safety. Hell of a thing. Haven't been able to move my arm hardly at all since. Hand's gone numb. Nothing to worry about, it's only a temporary cramp, but it's rather an inconvenience."

Finn thought that only an Englishman could speak in such an offhand manner about holding a man's life between his thumb and forefinger for three hours while under heavy fire.

"Anyway, it's nice to have you chaps," said Hugo, putting a cigarette in his mouth and awkwardly trying to strike a light with his left hand. Finn lit it for him. "Thank's, old boy. Didn't quite think you were riding into such a damned mess, did you?"

"Oh, I knew it would be bad," said Finn, "but it's another thing to see it. There must be thousands of them up there. It looks like the whole mountain range is on fire."

Hugo nodded. "More arriving every day. Word has it the Utman Khels have joined the fray. The Mahsuds, as well. The Mad Fakir's pulling them in. Final bloody conflict and all that. There're lathered up right and proper."

"They let us ride right in," said Finn.

Hugo nodded again. "Why not? Why take you in the open where you can make an effort at deploying? Better position here. Nothing short of a mass suicidal assault would break into this fort—not that I think they're not up it, mind you—but they have us trapped in here. It's like sitting atop a sugar cube in a great big empty cup. And they're all around the rim. I believe they're building up to final push. Meanwhile they continue sniping at us from the cliffs. They're damned proficient at it too. Bloody good marksmanship, at this range."

"Has there been any communication with Chakdarra?" Finn said.

"We managed to reestablish heliograph signaling with them briefly on the morning of the twenty-ninth," said Hugo. "They're hanging on, but they've sustained heavy losses. It seems they've had a rougher go of it than we. Food and ammunition are running short. Lieutenant-Colonel Adams took the Guides to make a try for the Amandara Pass, but they were forced to retire. He lost sixteen men and twenty-six horses. Now that you lot have arrived, we might stand a better chance. I was forced to miss the officer's conference. Had to tend to the wounded. Couldn't do much with this arm, you know. Stiff as bloody blazes. That new doctor was a godsend." He chuckled. "Godsend. Missionary, godsend, that's good, what?"

Finn smiled.

"So what's the plan, then?" Hugo said.

"General Blood's ordered the relieving column to assemble on Gretna Green there," Finn said, pointing. "The first attack will be directed toward Castle Rock, which dominates the high ground above the green. We move at half-past four this morning."

"Bloody hell," said Hugo. "If Castle Rock is taken at the same time as troops begin a push from Gretna Green, it might open up the graded road, and then deployment would be possible! Who thought of that?"

"General Blood."

"Now that I see it, it's so damned obvious," said Hugo. "But then, we hadn't the manpower before. We may get out of this mess yet. Well, I'd better go and give the good Father a hand." He held up his one useful arm and chuckled. "A hand, eh? That's a good one." Chuckling, he went down below.

Delaney hadn't had a chance to speak with either Lucas or Andre since their arrival. Tending the wounded at the garrison was a full-time job, especially with Hugo being limited in what he could do until his arm recovered from the cramping effects of his heroic action of the day before. All things considered, the morale of the troops at the fort was astonishingly high. They had been engaged in almost ceaseless fighting for a week, with little opportunity for sleep, and they were all exhausted, but they were functioning superbly.

As soon as the relief column of infantry had arrived, their officers had been ordered into conference with

General Meiklejohn and General Blood to make plans to break out and rescue the Chakdarra garrison. In a few hours the column would assemble and prepare to move while the attack against the overlooking rock formation commenced. Once the objective had been taken, Blood would then take up position with his staff upon the heights of Castle Rock, which would give him a commanding view of the field of battle.

Historically, Finn knew the tactics were to succeed and the column would break through to relieve the embattled fort at Chakdarra, but that would only be the start in a large operation that would last for months, culminating in the Tirah Expeditionary Force, a punitive action, launched against the Afridi homeland in the high mountain valley of Tirah. In between there were plenty of opportunities for things to go wrong.

Delaney knew that they had situated themselves as best they could under the circumstances, but this mission gave them less freedom to act than any other mission he had served. There was no chance now of breaking away from the troops to reconnoiter the situation in the hills. The cliffs were crawling with Ghazis. The best they could hope for was to stay with the main body and look out for any potential disruptive actions. Blood had to be protected at all costs. Meiklejohn as well. The main problem was that they didn't know who or where the enemy was—if, in fact, there was an enemy. Finn hoped there was. Fighting an enemy was easier than trying to compensate for an historical anomaly that might have been triggered by any number of events.

"I see you couldn't sleep either," said Churchill, coming up to stand beside Delaney. He looked out at the fires on the mountains. "I think the entire garrison's awake."

"Everyone's too worked up to sleep," said Finn. "I

know our men are looking forward to some action."

"They'll have plenty of it," Churchill said. "If the Ghazis sweep down upon Gretna Green before the attack can be launched and the high ground secured, we'll all be in for it. I've been preparing my dispatches. I only wish there were some way to convey the magnitude of this sight." He gestured out at the campfires on the cliffs. "Words simply can't do it. There must be thousands of them up there. And I had thought our strength would intimidate them. Private Mulvaney was right. My green is showing."

"Starting to regret having come along?" said Finn.

"Oh, not a bit of it," said Churchill. "It didn't appear as though the 4th Hussars were going to get in on any of this, and like any young fool, I was looking for trouble, I suppose." He grinned. "I seem to have found a good deal of it. Should make for some smashing reporting."

"Fancy yourself a writer, do you?" Finn said.

"More than mere fancy," Churchill said. "I'm already beginning to make something of an income at it, but I hope to do far better. True, I'm rather young, but then there's that fellow Kipling who's making such a big success, and he's not much older than I am. Still, he writes this romantic nonsense, and I have ambitions to do more serious work."

"Perhaps you'll be famous someday," Finn said, smiling inwardly at the earnestness of this serious young man. "Maybe this experience will turn into a book for you."

"I've already been giving that some thought," said Churchill. "Give the people back home some idea of what's happening here, more than merely dispatch writing—a detailed analysis of the Forward Policy and its effects, as well as of the military applications in carrying it out. Then perhaps the gentlemen MP's will know whereof they speak when they rise to address the Frontier Question on the floor of Parliament.''

"Sounds like a worthy ambition," Finn said, thinking that if the book were ever written, this youngster would probably find a way to make even the Malakand campaign seem deadly dull. To be so serious at so young an age! If the army didn't knock it out of him, he'd wind up a professor at a tiny college, or one of those ivory-tower historians forever buried in the stacks of some musty library. It seemed a shame. He was a nice young fellow. Here he was, in the midst of what would probably be the one great adventure of his lifetime, and all he could think of was the overall question, the grand perspective.

"You find the idea dull, don't you?" said Churchill, watching him intently.

"Well, no, I didn't say that—"

"You didn't have to," Churchill said. "It was clearly written in your face. I am an excellent judge of character. And I judge that diplomacy is not quite your forte. You're the sort of man who usually says exactly what he thinks."

"Well, now that you mention it, the way you put it did seem rather . . . well, rather dry," said Finn lamely.

"Dry," echoed Churchill. "Well then, I shall endeavor not to make it dry. I will see how my dispatches are received. If the reaction to what I write for the *Daily Telegraph* is not favorable, then I will not attempt to write the book. Rest assured, sir, I have too high a regard for the English people to subject them to inferiority. Good night to you."

In the fort's infirmary, Lucas and Andre had been working non-stop since the relief column arrived. The marksmanship of the Pathans had taken its toll in gaping holes and shattered bones from the lead balls fired by the jezails. The different calibers of the weapons produced a wide variety of wounds. The jezail rifles of the Ghazis were all handmade, some .45 caliber, some .50, some even larger, such as the .75 and .80 caliber "wall guns" which were either fired from bipods or from a rest position on a *sangar* wall.

Many of the wounds had been inflicted by captured British weapons, such as Martini-Henry and Lee-Metford rifles. The latter, which fired the new dumdum bullet, were particularly troublesome in the hands of the enemy. When one of these rounds hit a bone, it would expand, mushrooming out and tearing through everything in its path. If the victim wasn't killed, if the bullet struck an arm or leg, the result was usually the loss of that limb. Under the direction of Lieutenant Hugo, Lucas and Andre had performed a number of such amputations, and the infirmary was running dangerously low on morphia and chloroform. By nightfall both Lucas and Andre were exhausted. They could only imagine what it must have been like for Hugo.

"I think the two of you could do with some rest," the doctor said. "The most serious cases have been tended to, and the others will keep for a time. Besides, my arm's not quite so numb anymore and I can move it about some. I should be fit as a fiddle in another hour or so." He took a flask from his pocket. "There'll be more of the same tomorrow, I can guarantee you. Here, for medicinal purposes."

He handed them the flask and they each took a pull at it. "Thanks," said Lucas, sitting down in a wooden chair. He sighed. "I don't know how you've managed up till now."

"One does what one must," said Hugo, smiling tightly. "Perhaps now, after seeing all this, you can better appreciate your position, Father. There'll be no going out into the hills to preach the word until these hostilities are done with."

"That could take months," said Lucas.

"It could," said Hugo. "Meanwhile you're needed by your own. There shall be work aplenty for you two at Chakdarra, when we reach them. Speaking of which, Father, I think you should have this."

He handed Lucas a revolver.

"I can't take that," said Lucas, wanting to badly but knowing that staying in character meant he had to refuse.

"I'm not asking you to shoot anyone with it," said Hugo. "That will be a matter for your own conscience. But I've seen what happens when Pathans get hold of a man. They cut him to pieces or else take him back to camp and have sport with him there."

"I appreciate the gesture, Doctor," Lucas said, "but I couldn't possibly carry a gun."

"I can," Andre said. She took the revolver.

"Do you know how—" Hugo began, then stopped when he saw her quickly break the weapon open and check it. "Yes, I can see that you do. Useful skill for a woman to possess, especially in these parts. Well, go on now, you two. Get something to eat. You'll need all your strength tomorrow."

Sharif Khan received the emissaries in the main room of his house. Flanked by his chief bodyguards and lieutenants, TIA agents masquerading as Afridi tribesmen, Phoenix waited for the two emissaries to bow to him before he returned their greeting.

He noted that they carried ornate *khanjars*, tapering

eight-inch daggers with carved and inlaid hilts, as well as Khyber knives—the deadly *charras*—the long knives of the Pathans. The *charras* had heavy, single-edged, wide blades over twenty inches long which tapered gradually from the hilt to a sharp point at the end. The hilt, like those of the smaller knives, was without a guard, and had a slight projection on one side, by the pommel. The knives were encased in leather scabbards and worn thrust through the sashes, similar to the way Japanese samurai carried their swords. The men also carried the ubiquitous jezails, the curved-stock matchlock rifles which were frequently converted with captured English flintlocks. The barrels were long and slender, the stocks inlaid with silver plate. The weapons were as much a show of finery as force—the single most prized possession of an Afridi, when thus handsomely crafted, was evidence of wealth and status.

"The Most Holy, Mullah Sayyid Akbar sends greetings to the warlord Sharif Khan," said one of the emissaries. "He wishes to know why Sharif Khan has not responded to the call of the Prophet to rid our land of the infidel *firinghi*."

"Convey my most respectful greetings to His Holiness, Sayyid Akbar," said Phoenix, "and inform him that I have received no call to which I could respond."

The emissary looked at him with puzzlement. "Is the khan not aware of the flame that sweeps the land?" he said. "All the tribes are gathering for the Night of the Long Knives. The time is ripe to slay the invader. They are weak and powerless before the strength of the jehad. How can the khan be ignorant of this?"

"I have heard that the tribes were gathering," said Phoenix, "but there has been talk of the Great Jehad before. It is action that speaks loudest, and not words.

Sharif Khan does not blindly leave his holdings at the mere mention of a gathering of tribes. If there are spoils to be won, lives to be taken, that is another matter. But I have heard such talk before and little has come of it."

"Know this then, Sharif Khan," said the emissary, "that even as we speak, the infidel is being slaughtered in the Malakand by the forces of Sadullah, who speaks with the Voice of the Prophet. The Light of Islam, Sayyid Akbar, is now preparing to move against the British fortifications in the Khyber Pass. We strike everywhere and we strike as one. When comes the Night of the Long Knives, a great host shall come from the heavens to rid our land of the invader, and all who join in the jehad shall win their way to Paradise. Thus speaks Sadullah; thus speaks Sayyid Akbar. Where will Sharif Khan stand when comes the judgment? How shall Sharif Khan speak when it is asked who joined in the jehad and who stood by?"

"Does Sayyid Akbar question my faith?" said Phoenix.

"If the faith of Sharif Khan is beyond question," countered the emissary, "why does Sharif Khan refrain from joining in the holy war? We have heard much of Sharif Khan, of how he has quickly risen to the status of a warlord and of how his tribe, though smaller than some, has grown strong and prospered. Clearly Sharif Khan is among the chosen. It is only fitting for Sayyid Akbar to search out such a man and seek his aid in the great cause. It is the time for the chosen of Islam to join together and lead the tribes in the fight to force the invader from our land. This is the message Sayyid Akbar has sent. What reply shall we take back to him?"

"None," said Phoenix. "I will choose from among my tribe men to stay and watch over my holdings. Then I shall gather my warriors and return with you to deliver my reply to Sayyid Akbar myself. Sharif Khan has spoken. You will await my preparations and we shall depart together. In the meantime, let my humble home serve as your shelter. My retainers will see to it that you are made comfortable and that your hunger is appeased. You have been many days upon your journey. Rest and refresh yourselves, and then we shall begin our return.''

The emissaries bowed. "Sharif Khan is most kind and gracious. We shall humbly await your pleasure.'' Respectfully, they backed out of the room.

"This is what we've been waiting for," said Phoenix to his fellow agents when the emissaries had left. "If we're going to learn anything, we must be at the center of events. Three of you will remain here—Python, Zebra, and Mustang, keep the patrols going and report to me at once if you discover anything. If we need to send for reinforcements I'll communicate with you, and one of you will clock to Plus Time and report our findings. Agents Fox and Sable, you'll accompany me to Sayyid Akbar's camp. We'll leave a force of thirty men behind to conduct patrols and maintain security. The rest of the tribe, with the exception of the older men and women and the children, will travel with us. Any questions?''

"Just one," said agent Python. "There's supposed to be an adjustment team from the First Division back here somewhere, infiltrated into one of the British army regiments. We're assuming a cover with the other side. How do we keep from killing them if we all wind up in the same battle?''

"Unless there's some way you can recognize them, you don't," said Phoenix. "There's nothing to be done about that. There's a massive disruption going on back here, and we've got to get a fix on it somehow. Everything else comes secondary. Don't forget that if we can't keep from shooting at them, they can't keep from shooting at us as well. That's what happens when you've got teams on opposing sides. It comes with the territory. They knew the risks when they enlisted. So, for that matter, did we. Let's just try to survive this one, okay? It's liable to get pretty hairy. Any more questions?''

There were none.

"Right. Let's get the show on the road. We've got us a holy war to fight."

6 _____

Sayyid Akbar did not look like a holy man. Instead of white robes, he wore loose-fitting black trousers, high boots, a black shirt with flowing sleeves, and a black vest ornately embroidered in gold. His black turban was fastened with a ruby clasp. He towered over the white-garbed Sadullah as they stood in the Mad Mullah's tent high in the cliffs above the Malakand fort.

"I have done everything you asked of me, O Holy One," Sadullah said, his voice sounding very different from the way it did when he addressed his followers. It held a tone of abject supplication. "Even now, we have the British troops who have arrived trapped with the others in the fort. At dawn we shall strike and wipe them out to the last man! Then we will move to finish off the soldiers at Chakdarra."

"And what of the force assembling below, upon the green?" said Sayyid Akbar.

Sadullah smiled. "So much the better. My sentries have reported this to me. They think to attack the Buddhist Road. It is a foolhardy plan. They will be completely vulnerable to our fire from the high ground.''

"Have you bothered to gauge the size of this force?" Sayyid Akbar said.

"It is insignificant," Sadullah said. "Our own numbers are far greater."

"You're a fool, Sadullah," Sayyid Akbar said. "You have already lost this battle once before, and now you shall lose it again. I have given you another chance, and you are wasting it."

"But how have I failed, Holy One?" Sadullah said, chagrined. "I hold the British in the palm of my hand!"

"And they shall slip right through your fingers," Sayyid Akbar said. "It is pointless. You will never understand strategy. Never mind. It matters little to me if you do not destroy the British here, so long as you engage them. It will distract their attention from the Khyber Pass long enough to buy me the time to do what I must do there."

Sadullah's eyes were bright with the light of fanaticism. "The Night of the Long Knives? You will call forth the host of heaven?"

"They will come when it is time," Sayyid Akbar said. "When you have done all that you can do here, join me at my camp above the Khyber Pass."

"And then we shall strike?" Sadullah said.

"Then we shall strike," said Sayyid Akbar.

He vanished. The Mad Mullah prostrated himself upon the ground, weeping with joy. Surely he was blessed, he thought, anointed by the Prophet. The Holy One had been sent to deliver Islam, and he had been chosen as His instrument. Once before, he had launched the great jehad, and he had failed, not having anticipated the great strength and numbers of the British. The Holy One had turned back time and given him the chance to try again. He would not fail. At dawn his forces would descend upon the infidels and cut them to

pieces. Then he would take his followers to the Kyber
Pass to witness the coming of the host of heaven, before
whom the infidel *firinghi* would not stand a chance.
They would drive the invader from the land once and
for all, and for centuries to come the mullahs would
speak of how Sadullah the Anointed had prevailed and
won his way to Paradise. He pressed his forehead to the
ground and prayed with all the fervor of his soul.

As the first light of dawn showed above the peaks,
General Blood gave the order to advance. The force
assembled on Gretna Green immediately moved off
down the graded road in fours formation, while the
troops mobilized to attack the high ground set off under
the command of Colonel Goldney. Three hundred men
crept toward the *sangars* the Ghazis had erected upon
the cliffs of Castle Rock. The sentries, who had been
watching the assembled troops below, upon the green,
were taken by surprise. The troops came within one
hundred yards of their objective before they were
spotted and the enemy opened fire.

Goldney ordered a charge. Spreading out and moving
in from opposing flanks upon the *sangars*, the men
scrambled up the rocks, firing at will and engaging the
Ghazis at bayonet point. Surprised, and with no one to
direct their movements, the Ghazis gave ground before
the furious assault and the ridge was captured, completely without losses. Even as Sadullah was preparing
to order his Ghazis into action, the first engagement of
the battle was over and Castle Rock was captured.

Lucas and Andre watched with General Blood and his
staff from the heights of Castle Rock as the British
troops below pressed home the advantage of surprise.
The infantry fixed bayonets and advanced into the
Ghazi ranks. Without enemy fire from Castle Rock im-
peding their movements, they were able to deploy and

press their way through. So quickly had Goldney's men captured Castle Rock that the troops down below were already deployed and in position to force open the passage before the Ghazis knew that Castle Rock had fallen. By the time they realized what had happened, it was too late.

The assaulting troops charged into the Ghazi ranks. The Ghazis panicked and began to flee. As Sadullah watched in disbelief, his followers broke ranks and ran, scrambling from the rocks, where they were suddenly vulnerable to fire from the troops on Castle Rock. They took flight down the graded road to escape being trapped by their own numbers in the narrow pass.

"No!" Sadullah screamed uselessly. "Stand and fight! Stand and fight, you cowardly dogs!"

But his words were lost upon the wind.

"We've done it, General!" said Hugo, standing beside Blood and watching the enemy in full flight. "We've broken through! We can post pickets in the pass and reinforce our position. Now we can—"

"No," said Blood. "I will not allow them to escape so they can join with the tribesmen at Chakdarra and warn them. We'll finish this here and now. They'll be on the plain once they have retreated through the pass. Fully exposed and on foot. Order forth the lancers. No prisoners. No survivors."

The signal was given and the four squadrons of cavalry charged. Delaney, leading the second squadron of Bengal Lancers, couched his lance and leaned forward slightly, bearing down upon the fleeing Ghazis before him. It was going to be a slaughter. The tribesmen still trapped in the pass were run down and trampled by the lancers as they thundered through. The cavalry formed a line upon the plain and charged the fleeing enemy. There was no escape. The Ghazis died in the rice fields, run through by the lances and hacked to death by sabers. Bodies fell everywhere as the lancers descended on the running Ghazis and butchered them.

"Christ," said Hugo, turning away from the carnage down below. "I'm sorry, General, but that's more than I can stand too watch. I've seen enough of death."

Churchill was riveted by the spectacle. "They shall not forget this," he said. "It's probably the first time any of them have seen what cavalry can do, given room to deploy their strength. Henceforth the very words Bengal Lancers shall strike terror into their hearts."

He turned away and walked toward Hugo. At that moment one lone Ghazi who had remained undiscovered, hidden behind the rocks of his crumbled *sangar*, rose to a kneeling position and brought his jezail to bear upon Hugo, whom he took to be the commander of the British forces. As he raised his rifle, Lucas spotted him.

"Hugo, look out!"

Instinctively, after so much time spent under enemy fire, Hugo reacted by throwing himself down flat upon the ground. In an instant, Lucas saw that Hugo's combat-quick response had placed Churchill directly in the line of fire. In the white heat of adrenaline-charged clarity, he saw it all. He made a running dive for Churchill. The Ghazi fired. The .50 caliber ball slammed into Lucas's chest, ploughing through the thorax and tearing everything in its path. Andre fired the revolver Hugo had given her, shooting the Ghazi right between the eyes.

Churchill stood, shocked, staring at the limp body at his feet. Lucas Priest lay facedown upon the ground, blood draining from the gaping hole in his chest. "My God," he said.

He crouched down over the body and gently turned it over. The others gathered round.

"Doctor, can't you do something?" Churchill said.

Hugo looked down and shook his head. "I'm sorry,

son. There's nothing to be done. He saved my life, and then he gave his to save yours. And all he came here for was to preach the word of God.''

Andre got down on her knees and gently stroked Lucas's forehead. "No," she said, softly, "he came here to do much more than that."

She looked at Churchill, kneeling opposite her. He looked up at her, stricken. She looked back down at the lifeless body of her friend. She reached out and touched his face. It was still warm. She trailed her fingers across his forehead and closed his eyes for the last time.

They stood silently over the grave. General Blood had read the words, and when they had all said "Amen," Churchill had added a heartfelt, "Rest in peace, Father."

He won't do that here, Finn thought. When this is over, Search and Retrieve will disinter the body and return it to the time where it belongs. And another name will be added to the Wall of Honor at Division Headquarters, with a posthumous commendation.

He could not believe it. He had seen men die in combat throughout all of history, but he could not bring himself to accept that Lucas could be one of them. They had been through so much together, had faced death a hundred times and laughed about it later. There would be no laughing anymore. No more bouts of drinking Irish whiskey in the First Division lounge to wash away the taste of the last mission and celebrate having completed it successfully. No more brawling in the dives of San Diego and Ensenada, no more quiet nights spent with the old man in his private sanctum, sipping ancient wine as they talked about old missions.

The relief force was departing for Chakdarra. The job for them had only just begun. After the brief service, Blood had ordered Andre back to Peshawar, from there to depart for Simla, and preferably from Simla to England—which was home to her, so far as the general knew. He felt that the Father's death was his responsibility, that he never should have allowed him to accompany the unit in the first place, that if it wasn't for the fact that medical aid was sorely lacking, he would have been firm from the beginning. The frontier was no place for civilian noncombatants.

Finn was to head up a small detachment that would escort Andre back to safer territory and deliver dispatches to be sent on from Peshawar. Mulvaney, Learoyd, and Ortheris would be among those to accompany them, since they would have to ride and Blood didn't feel that he could spare any of his lancers. The cavalry had proved to be of great value, and he needed all the experienced horsemen under his command. Sending back one officer—the one with the least experience on the frontier—and several foot soldiers who could ride after a fashion, was the wisest choice. It would still be a hazardous journey, but one small mounted unit could move quickly and stood a better chance of getting through. All the tribes in the vicinity were up in arms, and most of them could be expected to join the forces at Chakdarra. There was far less risk in taking the opposite direction.

"I should have taken that bullet," Churchill said. "I am a soldier whose duty is to die for queen and country if the need arises. He was a man of God who would not even carry a gun."

He was about as far from being a man of God as a man could get, thought Finn. His duty was to die, as well, if the need arose. He had discharged it. His death was not for nothing.

"It's over then," said Finn, when they had gone. "We've done what we've come back here to do. Or Lucas has. Churchill will live now and go on to become prime minister of Great Britain. Ironic, isn't it? We came here to find a disruption to adjust, and it found us."

"Something's wrong," Andre said. "If I could think straight, maybe I could figure out what the hell it is, but I can't manage to do that now. All I know is that something's wrong. It isn't over yet. Maybe we should have remained with the field force."

"Not much chance of that, after Blood ordered us back," said Finn. "Besides, I don't know what the hell we should have done or should be doing. I just don't know anything anymore, and I don't much care either."

"You didn't remember Churchill before I told you about him, did you?" said Andre.

"What?"

"Lucas was going to talk to you about that, but he never got the chance. When we first met Churchill, I didn't remember him. I didn't know anything about him. But Lucas remembered him."

"Lucas was always a history addict," Finn said. "He used to say that you never know when you might need information that would help you . . . stay alive," he finished lamely.

"Then you knew?" said Andre.

"Knew about what?"

"About Churchill," Andre said. "That he would become prime minister of Great Britain."

"What are you talking about?" said Finn, angry with her for thinking about Churchill when Lucas was dead. "To hell with Churchill. Churchill's not an issue any longer. Whatever happened to begin the chain of events which led that Ghazi tribesman to kill Winston Churchill, whichever act interfered with history to bring that about, it's been compensated for, Lucas did it. I wish it had been me, but I wasn't even there. Damn it, I wasn't even there!"

"Finn," said Andre, softly, "I didn't know him as well as you did or as long, but I didn't love him any less. He thought this was important. I didn't know Churchill would become prime minister of Great Britain because there was nothing about him in the subknowledge of my implant education. There was nothing about him in the mission programming either. But Lucas knew. Lucas remembered. He didn't know it from his subknowledge, and he didn't know it from the mission programming. He just *remembered*. Do you understand?"

Delaney simply stared at her.

"Finn, you had to have encountered Churchill before Lucas died. You must have seen him at the officer's conference at least. Think, Finn, did you know who he was? Who he would be?"

"Of course I knew," said Finn, frowning. "I even had a chance to talk with him for a while last night. Hell, I remember thinking that he was so serious for his age, that if he didn't . . ."

"What?"

A blank look came over Finn's face.

"That doesn't make any sense," he said. "How could I have thought . . ." His voice trailed off.

"You didn't know him either, did you?" Andre said. "His name didn't trigger any responses. It was the same with me. It was the same with Lucas, too, don't you understand? Lucas remembered who Churchill was, but not because the information was contained in his subknowledge or in the mission programming. He remembered *reading* it. If Churchill was important enough to have been written about in history books, how could he have been left out of the implant education programs? How could there have been nothing about him in the mission programming if it was a known historical fact that he served in this campaign?"

"You're right," said Finn. "It wasn't in my subknowledge, either. After you told me what Lucas said, I just assumed—Wait a minute. If a historical disruption somehow brought about Churchill's death—if he actually caught that bullet—then that would have accounted for there being nothing about him in the implant education programs or in the mission programming, because he would never have survived to become prime minister of Great Britain. But then how could Lucas have read about him in history books? There must have been some sort of flaw in the mission programming."

"And in the implant education programs?" Andre said.

"I admit that sounds unlikely, but—"

"Sahib Finn?"

They turned around to see their native attendant, Gunga Din, approaching hesitantly.

"Yes, Din, what is it?" Finn said.

"Soldier sahibs say time to leave for Peshawar," said Din. "Mulvaney Sahib say must not waste daylight."

"He's right," said Finn. "Have you made everything ready, Din?"

"Everything ready," Din said. "Sahib Finn? Is permitted for this worthless one to pay respect Father Sahib?"

"Of course it's permitted, Din," said Finn.

Din approached the grave and stood over it for a moment, his lips moving as he silently said a prayer in his native tongue. When he was finished, he glanced at them with an embarrassed smile and thanked them profusely.

Finn knelt down over the grave and placed his hand upon the mound of earth. "Good-bye, old friend," he said.

They turned and walked away. Din, too, felt the loss. Perhaps he did not feel it so profoundly as did Finn and Andre, but he was overcome with emotion at the death of the one man who had ever treated him as something more than what he was—an untouchable. As they walked back down toward the green, Din glanced over his shoulder for one last look at the "Father Sahib's" grave. He squinted, blinked, then shook his head. He thought he had seen something, but there was nothing there now.

For a moment, just the barest fraction of a second, as he looked back up toward the knoll where the cemetery was located, Din thought he saw someone standing over the grave. Perhaps, thought Din, it was only his imagination. Or perhaps it was a portent. He shut his eyes and muttered a quick prayer to Shiva. He thought he had seen a tall, dark figure, wearing a long robe that billowed in the wind.

Sayyid Akbar stood high upon a precipice overlooking the Khyber Pass. Beyond, stretching as far as the eye could see, was the tortured landscape of the Himalayas, like giant rocky waves frozen into immobility. Below, at the bottom of the gorge, was a narrow, twisting trail, walled by sheer cliffs and broken by huge boulders. One small step forward would take him to oblivion, an oblivion he sometimes longed for. He had lived for a long time. The pathetic madman named Sadullah believed him to be a god, an incarnation of the Prophet or some minor deity of his absurd religion, but who knew? Who knew what twisted thoughts that passed for cogitation flashed through that demented mind? There was no need to understand him, so long as Sadullah could be used. And he was used so easily. As I am being used, thought Nikolai Drakov, whom Sadullah knew as Sayyid Akbar.

In a few months it would be his birthday. He would be ninety-three. He looked thirty-seven. His body was in peak physical condition, and his youthful face was marred only by the knife scar that ran from below his left eye to just above the corner of his mouth. In his costume as Sayyid Akbar, he looked like a dashing bandit chieftain, but he felt old. Emotionally drained. They had done that to him. Drained him. Leeched from him everything he knew. And now he could not exist without them.

As the sun rose above the peaks, thinning the mist, he looked down into the velvet-shrouded gorge, toward a narrow section of the pass hemmed in by two protruding rock formations. Like the Pillars of Hercules, he thought. The pillars that guard the gates. Three shapes stepped out of the undulating mist, walking out of one world into another. They looked up at him. He raised his arm to signal them.

The three figures rapidly ascended toward him from the bottom of the gorge, rising up until they were level with him and continuing on over his head to land behind him. He turned around as they shut off their jet-paks.

"Give us your report," said one of them.

"Everything proceeds according to plan," said Drakov. "The British are heavily engaged in the Malakand and at Chakdarra. Sadullah is working the tribesmen up into a frenzy about the coming Night of the Long Knives. He'll lose the battle at the Malakand fort, and undoubtedly the British will beat him at Chakdarra, but that makes little difference. The British Raj is convinced the uprising is confined to that area and that all the tribes have flocked to join Sadullah, so they haven't realized that I've rallied the remaining tribes to my side here. The garrisons in the Khyber Pass have been deserted, and even Colonel Warburton's Khyber Rifles have gone over to me, convinced I am the Light of Islam. Warburton has been transferred back to Lahore. He's retiring and going back to England. Without him to lead the Khyber Rifles, it was a simple matter to get them to join the jehad. That's something it will take the British years to understand, that it isn't the Empire the natives give their allegiance to, but individuals. As Oscar Wilde said, it is personalities and not principles that move the age. Meanwhile, I have finally succeeded in recruiting the last remaining independent warlord in the region. A local chieftain named Sharif Khan. The pass is now completely under my control. I have well over 10,000 men in my *lashkar*, more than enough to overrun Landi Kotal and destroy all the remaining forts in our path. Your way is clear."

"We'll have to move quickly," one of the three said. "There's no telling how long this confluence will remain stable. There's no margin for error, Drakov."

"There will be none, at least not on my part," said Drakov. "Just see to it that you live up to your part of our agreement."

"You have no need for concern," said another of the three. "Considering what is at stake, it's a miniscule price to pay. And it gives all of us what we want. What we require. Your life is at stake as well as ours. The most important thing is that the British are kept ignorant of your strength in this area. They must not send more troops until we can mobilize."

"They won't," said Drakov. "Since the action at the Malakand Pass began, I've been intercepting all of their communications. The telegraph wires are all down and the only dispatches which get through are the ones I wish to get through. They still think they're dealing with a small uprising. By the time they realize that every tribesman in the Hindu Kush is up in arms, it will be far too late."

"Good. It's imperative that you control the pass. The sooner we can move, the better. We'll see you again when we're ready to cross over."

They switched on their jet-paks and descended into

the gorge, arcing down toward the two pillars. Drakov watched them until they were swallowed by the mist. If any wandering tribesmen had been watching, Drakov thought, the legend of Sayyid Akbar had just grown greater. They would speak of how the Holy One communed with spirits, and they would anxiously await the moment when the host of heaven arrived. And they will arrive soon, thought Drakov. But not from heaven.

7

They were traveling in the opposite direction from Chakdarra, where most of the enemy forces were concentrated, but they were still in hostile territory. To avoid drawing unwanted attention to themselves, they wore the white robes of the Ghazis over their clothing and wound turbans around their heads. Even from a short distance there was nothing to distinguish them from a roving band of tribesmen riding captured British horses. To help complete the disguise, they carried jezail rifles in addition to their own Martini-Henrys and armed themselves with *charras*, which like the clothing and the rifles, they had taken from tribesmen killed at the scene of the battle. Mulvaney carefully inspected Andre's appearance before they set out, and grunted his approval.

"It'll do," he said. "No one will take you for a woman in that getup. Now all we need is to smear a bit o' dirt upon our faces to darken up our skin, and the lot of us'll be able to pass as Pathans."

"Unless anyone gets close enough to see that red hair

stickin' out from beneath your puggaree," said Learoyd.

They adjusted Mulvaney's turban and set off down
the road to Peshawar. They traveled quickly and made
it through the first day of their journey without inci-
dent. They stopped to pitch camp in the shelter of a rock
formation which would hide them and their campfire.
Ortheris boiled some water for tea, and they watched
the shadows lengthen as the sun slowly sank behind the
peaks.

"What'll you do now, miss?" said Learoyd.

"I don't quite know," said Andre.

Learoyd nodded, watching as Mulvaney and Ortheris
saw to the horses with the help of Gunga Din. Finn was
scouting around, looking to see if their position was
vulnerable. They could afford to take no chances. They
would stand watch in shifts, with the exception of
Andre and Din, Mulvaney having insisted that it was
work for soldiers. Neither Finn nor Andre were in a
position to disagree.

"It was too bad about the Father," said Learoyd.
"Were you close?"

Andre nodded. "We'd known each other for a long
time. He taught me almost all I know. It's hard to
believe he's dead. I feel as if I've lost a relative. It's the
second time that's happened to me. The first time, it
was my brother. I never thought I could feel pain like
that again."

"I know what you mean, miss," said Learoyd, staring out into the growing darkness, the flames making
dancing shadows on his face. "I lost someone once, myself."

"A brother?" Andre said.

"My son," Learoyd said softly.

"I didn't know you had a wife," said Andre.

"I don't, not anymore," Learoyd said. "It was a long

time ago, when we first arrived in India. Bombay, it was. There was an outbreak of typhoid. My young son came down with it. I remember sittin' up with him all night, prayin' for the fever to break. It didn't, and he died. My wife never forgave me. She blamed me for havin' brought them to this godforsaken place, and placed the burden of responsibility for our son's death squarely on my shoulders. He was just five years old. She went into hysterics and raved at me. After that she became very quiet and never said two words to me. She went back to London. I never saw nor heard from her again. Some time later a piece of paper arrived, informin' me that I wasn't married anymore, and that was an end of it.''

"You were an officer," said Andre.

Learoyd looked at her with surprise, as if he hadn't actually realized he had a listener.

"Enlisted men don't bring their wives with them," she said.

"I was a captain in the 4th Dragoon Guards," Learoyd said. He shrugged. "It was a long time ago. Ages, seems like."

"What happened?" Andre said.

"Why am I an infantry private now, you mean? I was broken. I was in a bit of a state after she left me. My commandin' officer saw me sulking about and drinkin' too much. I suppose he meant to snap me out of it. Provoked an argument. Told me I was better off without the bloody bitch. It was the wrong thing to say to me, you understand, and the worst time to say it. I thrashed him to within an inch of his life. Took five men to pull me off him, otherwise I'm sure I would have beaten him to death. All things considered, my punishment could have been far worse. Circumstances were taken into account, that sort of thing. I couldn't remain with the Guards after that. I requested a transfer to an infantry regiment and it was expeditiously granted. As to the pain, well, it subsided after a while. After a while longer, it more or less went away. But the memory comes back every now and then." He took a pull from his flask. "We do not, fortunately, have an infinite capacity for pain. But we do remember."

He handed her the flask. "Join me?"

"Thank you, I will," said Andre.

"Do yourself a favor," Learoyd said. "When we reach Peshawar, you keep right on goin'. This country is no place for someone like you." He held up a hand to forestall her comment. "I don't mean to imply that you're not up to it. I mean that it's no place for you. No place for any of us. We don't belong here. We came here with our bloody empire and our bloody customs and our bloody rules, and we're tryin' to impose the whole lot on people who want no part of it. I wonder how the folks at home would feel if Sadullah brought his Ghazi army into London, if he came with a corps of mullahs to do missionary work and instruct good Anglicans in the ways of Mohammad. Made them all build bloody mosques, closed down all the pubs and put veils on all the women. We'd start our own jehad. The lads and I are here for the duration, but you, there's nothin' to hold you here. Go back to London, find yourself a nice bloke and get married. Have yourself some kids, and talk about all this with the ladies over tea. Go home before this land withers your soul."

"Has it withered yours, Chris?" she said.

He sighed. "Perhaps it has. I don't know if I could go back home now. I've been here too long. In London I'd likely wind up on Leicester Square with a tin cup. Soldierin' is all I know."

"You're an educated man," she said.

"That's neither here nor there. Soldierin' gets in your blood after a while. It changes a man. It's all fine and good for a young chap just commissioned. He can parade around in his full dress, impressin' all the girls. For a bloke like me, who's been out on the front, it's another matter. Your home becomes your barracks, your family the men you serve with. You begin to talk like them and think like them. If you spend any time on the frontier, you begin to go a little native. You go back home and it's another world. One that doesn't make much sense somehow."

He stretched out his hand and she passed the flask back to him.

"It's a strange thing," he said, staring up at the rock walls towering above them. "I both hate and love this country. It isn't mine, you see, and it never shall be. Look at Din over there. He's got no home, but he's happy as a lark. He's got his soldier suit and he isn't an untouchable out here and that's all it takes to make him satisfied. Ortheris, well, Stanley doesn't much care where he is nor what he's doin' so long as he comes out of it okay. A more easygoin' chap you'll never meet. Mulvaney? If Terrence would have his way, he'd be back with the field force headin' for Chakdarra. He dearly loves a good, rousin' dustup. He's not truly happy unless he's putting his steel in someone's gizzard. In England he'd probably be in gaol. But me, I *think* about things far too much, so I look for trouble to keep my mind from thinkin'." He smiled. "As they say, it may not be much, but it's a livin'."

He handed her the flask. "Here, have another drink."

"What are we drinking to?" said Finn, returning with the others.

"Old times," said Andre.

Finn took out his own flask and unscrewed the cap. "I'll drink to that," he said.

"Old times," Learoyd said, holding up his flask.

"Old times," they echoed. They drank. And then a rifle shot cracked out. Ortheris fell to the ground.

The camp of Sayyid Akbar possessed all the atmosphere of a Kabul bazaar. It had engulfed the small cliffside village where it was situated, enlarging it many times. Tents had been erected not only all around the village, on all sides of it, but in the village streets as well. The thousands of tribesmen who gathered in answer to Akbar's summons made the camp festive and cacophonous. The mood was infectious. A great leader had arisen. The Light of Islam would rid the land of the hated British once and for all, and as the hoped-for day grew near, the fanatical enthusiasm of the tribesmen reached a fever pitch.

News of the siege at Malakand had spread quickly. There were as many different accounts of what had happened or was happening there as there were tongues. One version reported that the British garrison had been wiped out to the last man. Another claimed that the British garrison was being starved out. Still another story had it that the British soldiers were being decimated in ceaseless attacks by the faithful. The most popular seemed to be that the British soldiers had attempted to escape and were cut to pieces in the Malakand Pass. Sadullah supposedly had the head of the British commander on a pike. Sadullah himself had led the attacking forces, impervious to the bullets of the British. Sadullah was even now on his way to join Sayyid Akbar, the Light of Islam, bringing his thousands of followers with him. Together they would strike the final blow and call down the host of heaven to destroy the alien invader.

It was like a giant festival. Veiled women danced for the pleasure of the raucous mob. Horsemen played games of *buzkashi*, a savage Afghani version of polo in

which the "ball" was a freshly killed goat. The object of
the game was for the carcass of the goat to be dragged
across the goal line, and there weren't any rules beyond
that. It was a *juba*—a fair—in which the temper of the
throng possessed an ebb and flow, like tides, the noise
often rising to a deafening level.

In the center of the village was a large brick house
which Sayyid Akbar had taken as his headquarters.
Outside its walls a pit had been dug. It was deep and
square, with sheer walls of earth that made it impossible
for anyone thrown into it to climb out. The pit had been
filled with bugs of every description, so many that the
floor writhed with them. As Phoenix looked into it, he
saw that several unfortunate British soldiers, as well as
native tribesmen who had served in British regiments,
had been thrown into the bug pit. One of the men had
gone insane after who knew how much time spent in
there with inspects crawling over him. He screamed continually, ceaselessly trying to clamber up the sheer walls
of the pit, clawing at them with his ruined hands, much
to the amusement of the watching tribesmen. Another
of the men had died and his body lay in a corner, slowly
being devoured by bugs. The others were not far from
dead themselves. They expended what little energy they
had by constantly brushing off the insects. It was clear
that none of them had slept for a long time. Sleep in
such an environment was even more terrifying than
wakefulness.

"Poor bastards," Phoenix mumbled under his
breath. "Sayyid Akbar must be really something. It
takes a truly sick mind to come up with this."

"I've seen sicker," said agent Fox, standing close to
Phoenix. "But this one is right up there with the best of
them."

"There must be well over ten thousand men here,"

said agent Sable. "And if it's true that the Mad Mullah's coming here with his followers, that will make it at least twice as many. None of the garrisons in the area will be able to cope with a force that size."

"They didn't cope," said Phoenix. "Landi Kotal was overrun. It hasn't happened yet, but it will."

"Look," said Fox. He pointed to several men wearing khaki uniforms and turbans with red swatches of cloth in them.

"Khyber Rifles," Phoenix said. "Colonel Warburton's legendary native regiment. According to history it broke Warburton's heart when he found out his men deserted to the Ghazis. He trained them into the finest fighting force in the country, and this was his reward. Still, I wonder if you can really blame them."

"What does that mean?" Sable said.

"Put yourself in their place," said Phoenix. "You take service with a regiment whose duty is to keep the Khyber Pass open and to protect caravans from banditry. Suddenly you're faced with a war in which you have to fight your own people, not just bandits, but your countrymen, members of your tribe, maybe even blood relations. Worse, it's a jehad and there you are, a good Muslim, forced to fight against your own people in a war your faith tells you is a holy struggle to rid the country of infidel invaders. Invaders whom you serve. It has to tear you up. So you desert and get twice as fanatical and twice as savage as anybody else, to prove to them and to yourself that your heart was in the right place all along."

"I'd like to get a look at this Sayyid Akbar character," said Fox.

"You'll get your chance," said Phoenix. "I understand he grants an audience to each arriving chief and khan, along with his retainers. We'll be with the latest bunch that came in. We go in at sundown.''

"Sundown, eh?" said Sable. "Dramatic. What is this guy, a vampire?"

Phoenix glanced back at the pit. "After seeing that, I shouldn't wonder." He looked up at the sky. "It's almost time. Come on. Let's go pay our respects."

They joined the group gathered by the gates in the wall outside the house. Phoenix glanced up and saw that the gun tower over the house was manned. Sayyid Akbar was security-conscious. As the sun went down, the gates were opened to them and they went inside with a group of about twenty other tribal chiefs who had recently arrived. They crossed the small courtyard and went into the house, into the large central chamber which was decorated with tapestries and silk hangings. A number of lamps had been lighted to give the room a soft, dim illumination.

They were directed to wait at one end of the room, opposite a platform with a throne upon it, made from wood covered in hammered gold and silver. As the last rays of the sun disappeared, a group of heavily muscled guards came in to stand between the platform and those who had come to attend the audience. The men were armed with captured British Martini-Henry rifles, as well as officers' Webley-Wilkinson pistols. They all had *charras* tucked into their belts, along with smaller knives.

"On your knees before the Light of Islam!" one of them called out. Sayyid Akbar appeared seated on the throne, materializing out of thin air. Amidst the shocked reaction, agent Sable whispered to Phoenix, "A warp disc! We've hit the jackpot!"

They dropped down to their knees, touching their foreheads to the floor. Phoenix raised his head slightly, staring at Sayyid Akbar intently.

"Arise, my faithful ones," Akbar said in a deep, rich baritone.

"Drakov!" Phoenix said under his breath. He kept his head lowered, hoping Drakov would not get a good look at his face.

"I am Sayyid Akbar," said Drakov. "I have come to join with you in the Great Jehad." He got up and approached them, flanked by his bodyguards. "The time has come for the faithful to arise and throw off the chains of the invaders. The infidel *firinghi* has come to our land, seeking to claim it as his own. He comes seeking to expand his empire and to enslave us. He comes with arms to subjugate us. He comes with missionaries to attack our faith, seeking to make us infidels like himself. He comes to change our way of life, to take our land, to make us join his soldiers and to deny us Paradise. In so doing, he has raised our wrath and he has raised the wrath of higher powers."

His piercing gaze took them all in as he came closer, establishing magnetic eye contact with each man as he spoke.

"This day we are all one. Afridi, Mahsud, and Waziri; Yuzufrai, Mohmand, and Utman Khel; Swati and Orakzai—all joined together in the holy cause to fight for freedom. Today we are all Ghazi. Today we are *mujahidin*—holy warriors of the Great Jehad!"

He was coming closer. Phoenix kept his head down.

"The day is close at hand," said Drakov. "When next the moon is full, it will be the Night of the Long Knives." His hand closed around the jewel-encrusted hilt of his *charra*. "On that night the gates of Paradise shall open. A great host shall come forth to fight with us in our holy struggle. The British forts shall burn and the flames shall be seen in their own homeland, so that they will know never again to—"

He paused, standing before Phoenix. As if with great humility, Phoenix kept his gaze averted, looking down at his feet.

"You," Drakov said. "What is your name?"

"I am called Sharif Khan, Holy One," said Phoenix.

"Look at me."

Slowly Phoenix raised his head, meeting Drakov's gaze. Drakov's eyes widened for a moment, then he gave a faint ghost of a smile.

"Take this man," he said. "He is a British spy."

The bodyguard were on them instantly. Fox and Sable found their arms pinned behind their backs before they could get their weapons clear, and Phoenix was seized, the sharp point of a *charra* at his throat. The other tribesmen began yelling, pulling out their own knives and threatening to cut the agents to pieces on the spot. Drakov raised his arms and silenced them. Slowly, theatrically, he lowered them.

"Leave this man with me," he said. "As for the other two . . ." He turned and nodded to his guard. Moving with lightning speed, two of the guards plunged their long knives into Fox and Sable. The agents never even had a chance to cry out.

They appeared like wraiths from the shadows all around them, gliding like ghosts out of the darkness. Ortheris lay upon the ground, clutching at his left shoulder. A voice called out to them in English, "Throw down your weapons and you will not be harmed! Resist, and you will all be shot dead where you stand!"

"Bloody hell," Mulvaney said, "that sounds like a bloomin' *Yank!*"

Finn and Andre stood rooted to the spot, stunned.

"There are twenty rifles trained on you," the voice from the darkness said. "You're more valuable to me alive than dead, but if you force my hand, I'll take the loss."

Finn dropped his rifle. The others followed suit. Andre lowered her revolver. As it fell from her fingers, she stared at Finn and said, *"It can't be!"*

The man walked forward into the firelight. He was dressed in Temporal Army base fatigues, but they were field gray instead of black, and the insignia were different, unlike any they had ever seen before. He wore a patch over one eye, and in his right hand, held a laser at his side.

"Lucas?" Andre said with disbelief.

"See to the wounded soldier," the man in the gray uniform said. Another man similarly dressed came into the light and crouched down over Ortheris. He removed a first-aid kit from his pack. Others now moved into the light, and they could see that there was only one other man dressed in gray fatigues. The others were all Pathan tribesmen.

"Lucas, it *can't* be you!" said Andre. "We buried you!"

"Did you? What a shame. I guess I'm late to my own funeral."

"Blimey!" said Mulvaney. " 'E looks enough like the Father to be 'is ruddy twin!"

"Finn?" said Andre, looking at him wildly.

"It isn't Lucas," Finn said slowly. "At least not *our* Lucas."

"Congratulations, Lieutenant. Or is it lieutenant? What *is* your actual rank?"

"It's lieutenant. Second Lieutenant Finn Delaney."

"And you?" he said to Andre.

"Sergeant Andre Cross," she said numbly.

"Sergeant?" said Mulvaney. "Would someone mind tellin' me what in bloody 'Ell is goin' on 'ere?"

"It would only confuse you, soldier," said the twin. "I apologize about your friend. It was meant to be a warning shot, but these tribesmen tend to get a bit overzealous. Keeping them in check can be difficult. I strongly advise you to cooperate so as not to provide them with any excuse to give in to temptation. I believe you're carrying dispatches. May I see them, please?"

"What dispatches?" said Mulvaney. "We were only escortin'—"

"Please, Private, don't waste my time. The dispatches."

"Do as he says, Mulvaney," Finn said.

"What manner of uniform is that?" Learoyd said as Mulvaney removed the dispatches from the saddlebags. "You're not British, surely."

The twin Priest smiled. "It's the uniform of a captain in the Special Operations Group of the United States Temporal Army."

"The *United States*?" Learoyd said. "I don't understand. What's your interest here?"

"That," said the twin Priest, "would take a bit of explaining. And frankly, I don't have the time. Let's have those dispatches."

Mulvaney handed them over.

The twin Priest glanced through them quickly. "Yes, well, I'm afraid we can't allow these to get through." He handed them to one of the other men. He glanced at Finn. "Interesting," he said, "but not completely unexpected. Paradox piled upon paradox. Zen physics run riot in the presence of a confluence. I assume from your reaction on seeing me that my counterpart was with your unit. Pity. I would have liked to have met him."

"What is he talking about?" said Learoyd.

"Not now, Chris," said Andre, the initial shock having passed. "What are you going to do with us?"

"Take you prisoner," said the twin Priest. "After all,

I have as many questions to ask you as I'm sure you have to ask me.''

"What about them?" Finn said, jerking his head toward the others.

"We'll bring them along, just to ensure your cooperation. I wouldn't expect commandos to be very cooperative by themselves, but with hostages, it might be different."

"Look 'ere," said Mulvaney, striding forward belligerently. "I demand to know just what in bloomin' blazes—"

The twin Priest signaled to one of his men. There were three sharp, hissing sounds and Mulvaney and Learoyd dropped to the ground. Din slowly backed away, eyes wide.

"You there!" the twin Priest said, pointing at Din. "Come here!"

Din froze, petrified with fear.

"They're not dead," the twin Priest said. "They've just been put to sleep for a while. You have nothing to fear if you obey instructions."

Swallowing hard, Din came forward. The twin Priest looked at him hard. He spoke to Delaney. "This one's not a soldier. He with you?"

"He's just a Hindu attendant we hired," said Andre. "He's no danger to you."

The twin Priest looked at Din uncertainly for a moment. "Perhaps. I think we'll bring him along, just the same."

He turned and spoke briefly in Pushtu to the Pathans, telling them that he was leaving one of his men in charge and that the British soldiers were to be brought to the temple unharmed or else there would be dire consequences. He then addressed the two commandos. "Your warp discs, if you don't mind. Carefully. Don't try anything or the others die."

Reluctantly Finn and Andre surrendered their warp discs. The twin Priest glanced at Din, who stood quaking.

"He doesn't have one," said Andre. "I told you, he's only a—"

"Search him," said the twin Priest.

After a thorough search yielded no warp disc, he was satisfied. "Right. Follow me."

They went off a short distance into the rocks, to a spot where three Afridis stood guard with one gray-uniformed soldier over a warp disc about the size of a dinner plate. It was large enough to generate a field that could transport a platoon of men at one time. They took up position around it, within its field radius, and the uniformed man activated it. The Afridis dropped to all fours, pressing their foreheads to the ground as the disc began to glow. A moment later they disappeared.

A thorough search had divested Phoenix of his weapons and his warp disc. He sat cross-legged on a small cushion in a room on the upper floor of the small palace. Two muscular, armed guards stood by the door behind him, *tulwars* held across their chests. Four guards flanked Drakov, two on either side. Under other circumstances Phoenix might have found the scene amusing, reminiscent of *The Arabian Nights*. Drakov reclined before him on an elevated, cushion-covered platform. They were surrounded by rich silks and tapestries. Incense made the air fragrant. Drakov smoked a water pipe, adding the pungent odor of latakia to the smell of burning incense.

Beautiful young girls with diamond nose studs, emerald and ruby ornaments in the centers of their foreheads, and bracelets of hammered gold and silver on their wrists and ankles, waited on them, gliding in and out of the room in their flowing, silky costumes, bringing them platefuls of fruit and sweetmeats. One dark-eyed young beauty lounged on a cushion by Drakov's side, staring at Phoenix as Drakov absently fondled her breast. It was a fantastic scene, surreal except for the horrifying image of the guards plunging their knives into Fox and Sable.

"You're not eating, Martingale," said Drakov in English, so that they could converse in privacy.

"Did you expect me to have an appetite?" said Phoenix.

"After all we have been through together, I certainly did not expect you to be squeamish. Or sentimentally moralistic. I should have had you killed as well, but that would have left a lot of unanswered questions. Our meeting like this only serves to prove what I told you once before, that our destinies are linked. I gave you a position of power and responsibility. You betrayed me. I would like to hear your reasons. What did the Time Commandos have to offer you that I could not?"

Phoenix snorted. "Sanity, for one thing."

Drakov's eyes widened slightly. "You truly think I am insane? Could an insane man have accomplished what I have?"

"It's been done before," said Phoenix wryly. "I could name examples, but I don't think you'd care for the comparisons. On the other hand, you might be flattered."

Drakov smiled. "You don't understand. That much, at least, is clear. I suppose that was my mistake. As a leader, I should have motivated my men, imbued them with a sense of purpose. I failed with you. As you can see, I have not failed with these." He swept his arm out to indicate the guards.

"What's it all about, Nikolai?" said Phoenix. "What are you trying to do here?"

"Finish what I began," said Drakov. "More to the

point, what the Timekeepers began and were never able to see through to the end. Before a new order can be established, the old one must be torn down, destroyed completely. That is the first principle of anarchism. As in the karmic cycle, death must come before rebirth. Only in this case the cycle has been interfered with. Mensinger's warnings went unheeded, and what he feared most has finally come to pass."

"The alternate timeline," Phoenix said.

Drakov raised his eyebrows. "You surprise me. I am forever underestimating you. How much do you know?"

"Only that temporal interference has resulted in massive fluctuations in the timestream," Phoenix said, "bringing about a confluence between two separate timelines. Where do you fit in?"

"I am an integral part of it," said Drakov. "I may even have helped bring it about. When your treachery caused my submarine base to be raided, I escaped along with Benedetto. We had a contingency plan. We had preset our coordinates to the 27th century, the last time period in which anyone would think to look for us. But fate had a surprise in store for us. Somehow we clocked forward into a different timeline, almost identical to this one, a virtual mirror image, only with some significant discrepancies. We did not realize this at first, which led us to make mistakes that resulted in our being apprehended. Their surprise was as great as ours. Both Benedetto and I were exhaustively debriefed. They wrung us dry to get information about this timeline, which they had been unaware of. What they learned from us explained a great deal about certain phenomena they were experiencing.

"They had a Mensinger as well," Drakov continued, "one very much like ours. Only they listened to him. They possessed the sanity to stop their Time Wars. But we have forced them to begin again by making war on them."

"What are you talking about?" said Phoenix. "No one's made—"

"What do you think happens when someone sets off a warp grenade?" said Drakov, "such as when Lucas Priest exploded one in 19th century Ruritania to break out of Zenda Castle?"

Phoenix frowned. "What are you getting at?"

"A peculiar temporal phenomenon occurs," said Drakov. "The chronocircuitry in a warp grenade, as I understand it, is designed to clock the surplus energy of the explosion through an Einstein-Rosen Bridge to the Orion Nebula, where it can do no harm. Correct? Eminently practical for military applications, one would think. You can focus the energy of a nuclear explosion with pinpoint precision while the major force of its destructive power is teleported elsewhere. Only such massive expenditures of energy are never totally predictable, especially when coupled with the delicate alignment of chronotransitions."

"Which means?" said Phoenix.

"It means, my friend, that this latest insane escalation of military weaponry has thrown off the chronophysical alignments of the bridges Einstein-Rosen Generators tap into. The people in the alternate timeline have been the unfortunate victims of this phenomenon. You have been waging nuclear war upon them."

"My God," said Phoenix. "That would mean . . ." His voice trailed off.

"Thousands have been annihilated," Drakov said. "Hundreds of thousands. And they never knew the reason for the holocaust. They had no idea who was behind it. Until now."

8 ————————————————

They clocked into a large, shadowy hall inside a dark, cavernous building. The atmosphere was dank and musty, with a feeling of great age. Massive stone columns supported a domed ceiling, and torches flickered in stone sconces. At the far end of the hall, atop a giant altar, was a huge obsidian statue of the goddess Kali, arms held out like an arachnid, skulls around her neck, tongue lolling. Their footsteps echoed on the stone floor.

"Where are we?" said Finn.

"In an old, deserted lamasery high above the Khyber Pass," said the twin Priest. "It used to be the temple of a *thugee* cult, which accounts for the statue and the grotesque carvings on the columns. It makes for a suitable base of operations. From below it's virtually invisible. An observer won't even spot it with field glasses unless he knows what he's looking for."

They saw a number of Pathan tribesmen standing guard and a few gray-uniformed soldiers moving about briskly, carrying equipment. They were taken to a small chamber, lit by portable lamps which generated their own power. There was a long table in the center of the room, with about a dozen chairs around it. Priest directed them to sit.

There were a number of soldiers in the room, all standing around the perimeter, watching them. A number of the faces looked unfamiliar, but Delaney spotted one he thought he knew.

"Bryant?" he said.

The officer looked back at him, deadpan.

"Bryant, but not Bryant," Finn said.

The officer gave him a faint ghost of a smile.

"Martin," said Andre, seeing another man.

The husky, bearded lieutenant gave her a brief nod.

"It's amazing," said Delaney. "A mirror-image universe."

"Not quite," said Priest. "But close." He walked up to Finn and pulled off his turban. "If you have a counterpart, I haven't met him." He turned to Andre and yanked off her turban. Her long blonde hair cascaded down.

There was a strange look on his face. "Tell me about the other Lucas Priest," he said. "What was your relationship to him?"

"We were a team," she said. "The three of us. Lucas was my friend."

"For what it's worth, I'm sorry he's dead. How did it happen?"

"He died saving a man's life."

Priest nodded. "As good a way to go as any, I suppose. I wanted very much to meet him. I'd heard a great deal about you three."

"From whom?" Delaney said, frowning.

Priest smiled. "From a man named Drakov."

"Drakov!" said Delaney.

"Nikolai Drakov arrived in our timeline escaping

from you. Exactly how he managed to arrive is a complex question which we'll save for the time being. He was unaware at first that he was not quite where he thought he was. As a result he made several mistakes which led to his arrest. Imagine his surprise, and ours, when we learned the truth. He was put through an exhaustive interrogation, the purpose of which was to learn as much about your timeline as we could. I use the term *we* generically. I was not personally involved. At least not at that point.

"The discovery of your timeline's existence explained a great many things for us. It also raised a number of extremely difficult questions. For a number of years we had enjoyed uninterrupted peace. Our history, it seems, paralleled yours very closely. We had a Professor Mensinger as well, only he was considerably more successful than his counterpart in your timeline. He managed to prove to the Council of Nations that temporal warfare could interfere with history. Consequently, a ceasefire resolution was passed and temporal warfare was abandoned. The temporal armies were redirected toward space colonization, which I understand you have not pursued as extensively as we have. We found other means of settling our conflicts. Not perfect solutions, admittedly, but that need not concern you.

"Several years ago, by our Plus Time reckoning, we came under attack. A colony transport fleet was almost completely annihilated while en route to its destination with new settlers in coldsleep storage tanks. The few surviving ships could give no indication of why they were attacked, from where, or even by whom. Not long after that, the city of Altaira on the colony world New Queensland was destroyed. Reduced to slag. Again, no indication of who launched the attack nor from where it came. Other, similar attacks followed, apparently without rhyme or reason. Sometimes populated areas were destroyed, sometimes uninhabited moons or planetoids, sometimes the explosions occurred in space. Yet they all had the same things in common. No one could tell who was responsible. No one could tell where the attacks came from. Each attack was a nuclear strike. And we have now learned that each attack came from your timeline, through an artificially created warp in spacetime.''

"Warp grenades," Delaney said in a low voice. "Sweet Jesus, what have we done?"

"Killed thousands, millions of innocent people," Priest said. "And, until Nikolai Drakov fell into our hands, we had no idea who was responsible."

"How could we have known?" said Andre in a shocked voice.

Priest shrugged fatalistically. "Perhaps you couldn't have. Your moral culpability, on purely ethical grounds, is certainly open to debate, but that's neither here nor there. Suffice it to say that while it may be understood, in principle, that you didn't realize what you were doing, a great many people don't see it that way. If you had known, I have no doubt you would have stopped teleporting nuclear explosions through corridors in spacetime that bridged to our universe. But would that have been enough? What about all the lives that were lost? How could you possibly make reparations for them? Besides, the situation is considerably more complex than that.

"I was in retirement when I was reactivated. I thought I had seen an end of military service, but there was a need for personnel with my qualifications. The Special Operations Group was brought together based on information obtained from Nikolai Drakov. One of my main objectives on this mission was to locate you. Not you specifically, but the temporal adjustment team we were certain would be sent back to this time period when a discontinuity became evident."

"You traced our warp discs somehow," said Delaney.

"It took a good deal of time," said Priest, "but that was to be expected. We weren't sure when you would arrive or where you'd be."

"And now that you've found us?" Andre said.

"First, I need to establish to my satisfaction that you two are the only temporal soldiers in the group. You were the only ones carrying discs, but I need to be sure. This one," he approached Din, who sat wide-eyed, totally bewildered by it all, "is probably exactly what you say he is, unless he's one hell of a damned good actor. The others I am equally disposed to believe are native to this time period. Scanning procedures will quickly establish that."

"And then?" said Finn.

"One of you will return with us for some rather extensive debriefing. The other one will be allowed to return to Plus Time—your own Plus Time, that is—with an offer of terms."

"What sort of terms?" said Andre.

"It should be obvious that unrestricted warfare between our two timelines would have devastating results for all concerned. It would be impossible to control. Neither you nor we would be able to target our weapons with any reasonable degree of accuracy. There are massive fluctuations in each timestream, resulting in points of confluence between our two timelines. That was how Drakov fell into our hands. The prevailing theory among our scientists is that discontinuities created by temporal actions in your timeline are responsible. The confluence effect may have been brought about by a single, massive disruption, or it could have been cumulative. The possibility was briefly considered that one of the two timelines was created by a timestream split, but fortunately that hypothesis was dismissed when we discovered significant differences in our histories and even in certain of our natural laws. I say fortunately because if that were not the case, we would be faced with certain insurmountable . . . philosophical questions, for lack of a better way of saying it. However, that still leaves us with other problems.

"We are confronted with the fact that you have committed hostile acts against us—knowingly or unknowingly, that's not at issue. We are also confronted with the fact that our timelines are intertwining in a completely unpredictable manner, like some cosmic double helix. Our scientists believe there's a possibility that our two timelines, as a result of interactive temporal inertia, could stabilize by merging into one. The results could be disastrous, on an unimaginable scale.

"Even without that possibility, our Council is still faced with overwhelming pressure. People want retribution for the destruction of the colonies. We don't have any choice in the matter. If interactive temporal inertia compensates for the instability of our timelines by making them flow together into a single timeline, then the only course of action open to us is to *maintain* that instability. Perhaps if the instability were magnified, temporal inertia would be overwhelmed and our timelines would be forced apart."

"*Perhaps?*" Delaney said. "There's no way of knowing that! What you're suggesting *could* work the way you say, but hell, that's only theoretical! It could also result in a massive timestream split!"

"That possibility was taken into consideration," Priest said. "Our scientists think a timestream split could serve to overcome the confluence effect. True, it would create a whole new, possibly more serious problem, but if the split took place in *your* timeline, it would create no difficulties for us.

"*We* were not responsible for this situation," he continued. "We foresaw the dangers and we stopped our Time Wars. You did not, and we have suffered for it, so we're not terribly concerned about splitting your timeline if that solves our problem. However, that may prove to be difficult. It may take some doing, so we'd like to negotiate a treaty—call it agreeing upon conventions of war—wherein both sides agree to limit the conflict to temporal actions. Otherwise the result would be incalculable loss of life on both sides from advanced weaponry which may, because of the confluence effect, become redirected at the user. The war is already a fait accompli. We merely wish to limit the potential casualties and wage it as logically as possible."

"*Logically?*" said Delaney. "*Do you realize what you're saying?*"

Priest nodded. "Unfortunately, Lieutenant Delaney, I realize only too well. I don't like this any better than you do, but I have no choice. We must interfere with your history in order to protect our own. We must increase the instability in your timeline, even to the point of bringing about a timestream split if necessary, in order to maintain our temporal integrity."

"A war like that would have disastrous consequences for both our timelines," said Andre. "There *has* to be another alternative!"

"There is," said Priest. "We'd like to avoid an all-out temporal war, if possible. The only way to ensure that is with a massive first strike. And that is my other objective on this mission. You are prisoners of war. You will be treated fairly, with the respect due to your rank. But I must warn you that any attempt to escape will result in execution. Lock them up."

The soldiers from the alternate timeline led them

away. Priest watched them go, a strange expression on his face. Captain Bryant came up to stand beside him.

"Well," he said laconically, "that certainly was interesting. I thought you handled that very well, considering."

"It wasn't easy," Priest said tensely. "I had to keep telling myself she's a different person."

"She's not, you know," said Bryant. "Her genetic makeup is the same. She looks the same, she talks the same—"

"Enough!" said Priest. "What are you trying to do?"

"I'm trying to make you face up to it now, before it really starts eating at your guts," said Bryant.

"She isn't the same Andre. She's *not* my wife."

"You and I both know that," Bryant said, "but we also know how you fell apart when your wife died. Lucas, don't do this to yourself. Let Martin handle the interrogation."

Priest shook his head. "We're all going to have to face up to this sooner or later. It's like making war upon ourselves. I can't delegate responsibility simply because I don't have the stomach to do what must be done."

"It's not the same thing," said Bryant. "I wish you'd reconsider."

"I wish I could," said Priest. "But I can't abandon my responsibility. When the time comes, I'll have to wring her dry. Meanwhile, I think I'll go get drunk."

"A fine thing," said Darkness, manifesting from his tachyon state. "I send you out to gather information and you get yourself jailed."

Phoenix quickly got his feet inside the cell. "Man, am I glad to see you! But keep your voice down, for Christ's sake! The guards will hear!"

"Of what concern is that to me? I have far more important matters on my mind. Have you managed to learn anything at all?"

"I've learned plenty. Come on, Doc, keep it down, you'll only—"

The door to the cell opened and a guard looked in. Seeing Darkness, he charged into the cell, his sword swinging in a sharp, descending arc. It passed right through the scientist.

"Get out," said Darkness. "I'm having a conversation."

The burly tribesman stared at him, bug-eyed. The other guard came running in and tried to grab Darkness from behind, only to have his arms close around empty air. The two tribesmen stared at each other in astonishment. From behind them Darkness said, "You two are beginning to annoy me. Phoenix, you speak their gibberish. Tell them to get the devil out of here."

"You'd better leave before you make him angry," Phoenix said to the guards in Pushtu. They fled, screaming.

"Well, that's all fine for you," said Phoenix, "but what do *I* do when half the Ghazi army comes running in here?"

"That's of no consequence to me at the moment," Darkness said. "We need to talk."

"Of no consequence to *you*? Now just a—"

"Don't interrupt. There have been unfortunate developments. Lucas Priest is dead. I homed in on his symbiotracer only to find a corpse. It seems he died saving Winston Churchill's life. A noble sacrifice, I must admit, Churchill wrote some excellent books. Still, there's the matter of your agents. I can find no trace of any of them. I must assume they were killed. The most logical explanation is that—"

There was shouting in the corridor outside the cell

and the sounds of running feet.

"We'll never get anywhere with these constant interruptions," Darkness said. "We'll have to continue this discussion elsewhere."

He translated into tachyons and disappeared from sight.

"Darkness! Wait!" shouted Phoenix.

A large group of heavily armed Ghazis burst into the room.

"Darkness, God-damn-you-lousy-son-of-a—"

An arm appeared out of thin air behind Phoenix. It grabbed him by the collar and yanked. Phoenix disappeared. The Ghazis trampled each other trying to get out of the room.

"—bitch!"

"Really?" Darkness said. "I should have left you back there to face those primitives."

"Holy shit," said Phoenix.

He looked around. He was in a large, cluttered laboratory with wall-to-wall computer banks and other electronic instruments. Dominant in the room was a huge radio telescope. The domed ceiling made the room an observatory. There was an incredible array of equipment, most of which Phoenix could not identify, and in a bizarre juxtaposition, scientific apparatus stood side by side with exquisite Victorian antiques, bronze sculptures, and oil paintings. Books were everywhere, in shelves upon the walls, stacked on desks and tables, piled on the floor. There were thousands of them.

"Where in hell *am* I?"

He turned and saw a large bay window. The landscape outside was rocky and desolate. It was also vermilion. He could see nothing but desert and rocks for miles. And he could see three moons.

"Doc?"

He turned around. Darkness looked drained. He

walked over to a large reading chair and collapsed into it.

"You can move!"

"Of course I can move, you imbecile."

"I mean, you can walk like a normal person!"

The scientist made a wry face. "Thank you. I assume you meant that as a compliment. Yes, I can indeed move about like a normal person, as you say, when I am not in transit in my translated state. In other words, I do not violate the Law of Baryon Conservation when I am home."

"Home?" said Phoenix. "You mean . . . this is *it*?" He glanced quickly back at the window, at the three moons in the sky. "Christ, we're not on earth!"

"Your powers of deduction are truly overwhelming," Darkness said. "There is a bottle of scotch on that sideboard there. Be so good as to pour me a glass. And help yourself as well."

The scientist looked exhausted. Phoenix swallowed hard, then moved to comply. "How the hell did you *do* . . . whatever the hell it was you did?"

"The scotch, Phoenix, the scotch."

Phoenix handed him the glass and Darkness tossed it down. "I won't try to explain *how* I did it, because I don't feel like talking for six hours. *What* I did was to extend my tachyon field for a brief interval and drag you into it. I discovered I could do that, briefly, without altering the molecular structure of objects, but it depletes my energy severely. It's quite an interesting phenomenon. Didn't know that I could do it with people."

"Wait a minute," Phoenix said. "You mean I'm the first person you ever tried that with?"

"Well, I've never had occasion to attempt it with a living being before," said Darkness. "The principle should be the same . . . the structure of molecules is, after all . . . you do *feel* all right, don't you?"

"I don't know. How would I feel if my molecules were out of whack?"

"That could be painful," Darkness said.

"Very funny. How do I know I haven't become like you?"

"*You* could never become like *me*. But I assume you're referring to an alteration in your molecular structure. Rest assured, it would take a great deal more than a brief exposure to my energy field to tachyonize your own molecular structure. However, if you find yourself leaving to go somewhere and arriving before you've left, I would say you may have some cause for concern."

"Just where exactly *are* we?" Phoenix said.

"We are in another galaxy," said Darkness. "That's all you need to know."

"I can't believe it."

"That doesn't surprise me. However, if you can manage to contain your incredulity, we have some things we need to discuss. Apparently the situation is a great deal more serious than I thought. With Lucas Priest dead, I have no way of finding the adjustment team. He was the only one of them who had one of my symbiotracers. And since your agents have all disappeared without a trace, I must assume the worst."

"Drakov had Fox and Sable killed," said Phoenix. "My cover was blown when he recognized me."

"*Drakov?* How does he fit into this?"

"He's leading the Great Jehad as Sayyid Akbar," said Phoenix, then quickly brought the scientist up to date on what he had learned. "The only reason he didn't have me killed was that he wanted to turn me over to the soldiers from the other timeline. Doc, according to Drakov it's an almost identical alternate universe. I wasn't able to learn very much about it, but Drakov claims it's enough like ours that he couldn't tell the difference at first."

"Interesting," said Darkness. "That may explain a great deal. I was wondering why the confluence effect did not manifest itself more profoundly. Perhaps it has and we simply haven't noticed it."

"How's that?"

"Well, think of colors, for example. Imagine a flowing river of red. Now imagine another river that's yellow. If they flow into one another, you'll have an orange river. But if both rivers are red to begin with, only of slightly different hues, you might not readily observe a graphic change in color as a result of the confluence. Similarly, given parallel timelines of an almost identical nature, the points of confluence between them might not be readily apparent. Small wonder I haven't been able to pinpoint them. I've been searching for dramatic fluctuations in temporal energy. Wrong method entirely. I should have been looking for anomalous inertial surge, instead. Of course. It seems so obvious, it should have occurred to me before."

"Doc, you're losing me again."

"Yes, well, you're lost to begin with. But then, I'm not much better. If I had foreseen this possibility, none of this would have happened."

"What do you mean?"

"I'm the one who invented warp grenades, remember?" said Darkness. He looked down at the floor. "I think I know now how the inventors of the atomic bomb must have felt. It never occurred to me that teleporting such massive amounts of energy through Einstein-Rosen Bridges could interfere with the chronophysical alignments of the warps. After all, there were already immeasurable amounts of energy involved, I didn't see how it could make any difference. The effects must have been exponential."

"Doc, you mind speaking in English? To tell you the truth, I really don't give a damn *how* it happened. It happened and now we've got to deal with it somehow. How about concentrating on that?"

"My friend, I've been thinking of little else."

"And?"

"And I haven't come up with anything. Not even Mensinger would have been able to solve this one. I suspect that's what drove him over the brink. He realized he had set in motion a chain of events that were bound to escalate out of control sooner or later. The people in the alternate timeline are faced with precisely the same problem, though admittedly that doesn't help us much."

"Only they're trying to do something about it," Phoenix said.

"Yes, well, they're obviously concerned about maintaining their temporal integrity," said Darkness.

"At our expense," said Phoenix.

"I can hardly blame them," Darkness said. "Clearly they're ahead of us in one respect. They've managed to pinpoint at least one confluence and use it to cross over into our timeline. If my supposition is correct, and the confluence point can be located by inertial surge . . ." He snapped his fingers. "Of course! *That's* what they're doing!"

"What?"

"The two timelines are dissimilar enough to cause instability in the temporal flow," said Darkness, "but the Fate Factor enters in at points of confluence and attempts to compensate, only since the timelines are not dissimilar enough to set up a crosscurrent effect that would manifest itself in discontinuities, the result is a surge in the inertial flow! We have instability due to the proximity of the two timelines, yet a stronger inertial flow at points of confluence. The greater the number of confluence points, the stronger the inertial flow. Eventually this magnified temporal inertia would have to overcome the instability, and the two timelines would merge into one!''

"You mean sort of like a timestream split in reverse?" said Phoenix, frowning.

"Not bad," said Darkness. "That's a very good way of putting it. Sometimes I underestimate you. You may be a little slow, but you do learn."

"Thanks," said Phoenix wryly. "But what does it all mean?"

Darkness shook his head. "I see I spoke too soon. Very well, let me put it to you this way: you're faced with a situation in which you are forced to choose between the lesser of two evils. On the one hand you have temporal instability caused by chronophysical misalignment, bringing two separate timelines too close together and causing them to intersect as a result of the interaction of their temporal fields."

"The confluence effect."

"Exactly. On the other hand this confluence effect causes a surge in temporal inertia at the confluence points, which affects both timelines simultaneously, increasing the confluence phenomenon."

"And if it keeps happening, you'd wind up with a single merged timeline," Phoenix said. "So in order to prevent that, you have to do something to reduce or eliminate the confluence effect."

"Correct. And?"

"And . . . and if the confluence effect is a result of the Fate Factor trying to compensate for temporal instability . . . you try to reduce the confluence effect by *increasing* the instability?"

"Bravo. We'll make a temporal physicist of you yet."

"But . . . that's crazy!" Phoenix said. "The more you increase temporal instability, the greater the chance of bringing about a timestream split!"

"Ah, but in *which* timeline?"

"The one with the greater instability?"

"Pour yourself another drink, lad. You've just hit the nail right on the head. A timestream split would be almost certain to overcome the confluence effect, and it could result in changing the chronophysical alignment between the two timelines, forcing them apart, in a manner of speaking. But that's only in theory. And it's only one possibility."

"What are the other possibilities?"

"Theoretically it could also result in *three* timelines experiencing points of confluence with an exponential increase in the instability factor. Then the same thing would begin all over again, only you'd have three timelines trying to achieve stability by merging into one. And in order to prevent that, you'd have to increase the instability again to a point where it would overwhelm the compensating influence of the Fate Factor, and you could wind up with yet another timestream split, resulting in *four* timelines, and so on ad infinitum. You'd be trapped in a situation where you'd have passed a point of no return and the only way to make it better, for the short term, would be to keep on making it worse."

"Jesus. Where would it all end?"

"You've got me. What's the absolute opposite of entropy?"

"I don't know. What?"

"I don't know either. Could be the Big Bang all over again."

"So what the hell do we *do*?"

"Dr. Darkness does not, alas, know everything," the scientist said, sighing heavily. "I must admit to a certain morbid fascination with all this. What an incredible opportunity for research. This could enable us to quantify Zen physics. We could be in a position to actually observe—"

"Doc!"

"What? Oh, sorry. You must forgive my enthusiasm. Occupational hazard. I'll try to keep a lid on it."

"So what's the answer?"

"What's the question?"

"What do we *do* we about this mess?"

"Stall."

"What do you mean, *stall*? How?"

"Well, since no clear-cut solution seems to present itself, the most we can do under the circumstances is to maintain the status quo as long as possible," said Darkness. "The people from the alternate timeline are obviously attempting to hit us with a massive temporal first strike, trying to cause a significant historical disruption that might lead to a timestream split in our own timeline. We must not only prevent that, we must strike back at them in the same way. They interfere with our history, we interfere with theirs; each of us tries to adjust for the disruptions and maintain the instability as long as possible while trying to preserve a reasonable amount of temporal integrity on both sides."

Phoenix stared at him, slack-jawed. "Are you serious?"

"I'm very serious. It doesn't solve the problem, admittedly, but it might keep it from getting worse. And it does have the added benefit of giving everyone a common enemy. No more temporal conflicts between nations. Everyone will be too busy fighting against the other timeline. It could have considerable domestic advantages. Now we'll *really* have a Time War on our hands."

"And just how long do we keep this up?" said Phoenix.

Darkness shrugged.

"Christ. I think I need another drink."

9 _____

They were taken to a large chamber in the temple and locked inside. The massive wooden door was thick, bolted, and reinforced with iron. There were no windows in the chamber, but light filtered in from the top of a short flight of stairs. There were two large, thick pillars in the center of the room, supporting the ceiling. The walls were mortared stone. Learoyd, Ortheris, and Mulvaney had already been brought there, but they were still unconscious. Gunga Din climbed the flight of stairs, and a moment later they heard him call out. They followed him up the stairs.

"Sahib Finn! Memsahib Cross! Look!"

The stairs ended on a parapet built out of the side of a mountain cliff. Below them was an abyss, a sheer drop to the bottom of the Khyber Pass.

"It's a long way down," said Finn.

"Looks like we're stuck," said Andre.

"Sahib Finn, how we come here? Who are these people?"

"I don't know how to tell you, Din," said Finn.

"They are demons!"

"No, Din, they're not demons. Just . . . powerful fakirs." He shrugged. How else could he explain it?

"They will kill us, yes?" Din said.

"I don't know."

"Soldier sahibs dead."

"No, they're not dead, Din. Drugged. They'll be waking up before too long."

"This place . . . Kali worship," Din said. "These men serve Kali. *Thugee*. Kill us all."

"We're not dead yet. Go keep an eye on Mulvaney and the others. They should be coming 'round soon."

Shaking his head in despair, Din shuffled back down the stairs.

"Finn, look!" said Andre.

She pointed down into the pass. Far below them two men appeared out of the mist, rising up toward them rapidly on jet-paks. They entered the temple through another chamber cut into the side of the cliff below them.

"That's how they're getting through," said Finn. "The bridge between the timelines must be down there."

"What about the British troops stationed in the pass?" said Andre. "What about the forts?"

"Undoubtedly taken over," Finn said. "Some of those tribesmen we saw in the main chamber were wearing khakis and turbans with red swatches of cloth in them. Khyber Rifles. These people have taken advantage of the jehad to get all the tribesmen on their side. The Ghazis must think they're gods or something."

"Finn, that's it!" said Andre, grabbing him by the arm. "According to history, Sadullah promised the tribes they'd defeat the British on the Night of the Long Knives, when the gates of Paradise would open and a great heavenly host would come forth to help them drive out the infidels." She pointed down into the pass. "That's where they'll be coming through. They'll fight on the side of the Ghazis, and the British won't stand a chance."

"It makes sense," said Finn. "While Blood was putting down the uprising in the Malakand, the Mad Mullah escaped and joined Sayyid Akbar in the Khyber Pass. They overran Landi Kotal and burned every fort in their path. Akbar demanded the withdrawal of all British forces. To stop him, the British sent the Tirah Expeditionary Force under General Sir William Lockhart. Their objective was to defeat Akbar and then strike at the tribes in the Tirah Valley. That crushed the revolt."

"Only with the soldiers from the other timeline fighting with the Ghazis, it won't happen that way," Andre said. "That's what he meant by a first strike. We thought Churchill was the focus of the disruption. It was never Churchill. It was the entire Tirah Expeditionary Force!"

"If they destroyed the expeditionary force," said Finn, "there'd be nothing stopping the Ghazis from sweeping down into Peshawar. The British control of the frontier would be eliminated, leaving the way open for the Russians to come in. And the Russians have already been negotiating with Abdur Rahman in Kabul. It would completely alter history in this part of the world."

"We've got to stop them somehow."

"I'm open to suggestions," Finn said. "We've had our warp discs taken from us, and even if we do figure out a way to escape, we have to make sure Mulvaney, Ortheris, and Learoyd get out with us. We can't just leave them here."

"What if there's no other choice?"

Finn grimaced. "Right now we don't have *any*

choices. Unless we can learn to fly, I don't know how we're going to get out of here. And we're running out of time."

"We have to find the point of confluence," said Darkness, pacing back and forth across his laboratory. "My instruments can only detect energy fluctuations in the timestream. They were never designed to pinpoint inertial surge. I might be able to find it if I'm on the scene."

"Then get me back to Earth in Plus Time," Phoenix said. "Somebody has to let them know what's going on. I can alert the TIA and the Referee Corps."

"No, you leave that to me," said Darkness. "The confluence must be located first. The best thing for you to do is concentrate on Drakov."

"We have a problem there," said Phoenix. "There really was a tribal leader named Sayyid Akbar. Knowing Drakov as I do, he probably killed the real one and took his place. That means we need him. Sayyid Akbar was a key figure in the scenario. His revolt in the Khyber was what caused the British to launch the Tirah Expeditionary Force. Without him—"

"Wait," said Darkness. "What about this expeditionary force?"

"They put down Akbar's revolt in the Khyber and then pursued a punitive campaign against the tribesmen in the Tirah Valley," Phoenix said. "It ended the uprising and—wait a minute! If the Tirah Expeditionary Force had been defeated, it could have ended British control of the frontier. It would have given the Russians a foothold. Control of the frontier would give them access to India. It could lead to a war."

"And a timestream split," said Darkness. "That's the connection. The Khyber Pass."

"And Akbar—or Drakov—controls the Khyber Pass."

"The confluence must be there," said Darkness. "It has to be, everything points to it. Our timing must be precise. We must allow Drakov and Sadullah to join forces and begin their Night of the Long Knives. We cannot act until the British have launched the Tirah expedition."

"What about Drakov?" Phoenix said. "When he finds out I've escaped, he'll know his cover's blown."

"Then they'll be prepared," said Darkness, "but they can't stop now. Too much rides on their plan. They're committed."

"There's still an adjustment team back there somewhere."

"The last place they were was at the Malakand fort. I tried to home in on Priest's symbiotracer, and as I said, only found his grave. The regiment had already departed for Chakdarra. I couldn't manifest because there were several other soldiers present. They were on their way to Peshawar with dispatches."

"None of the dispatches from the Malakand have been getting through," said Phoenix. "Drakov's tribesmen have been intercepting them."

"They could easily have teleported if they ran into trouble," Darkness said. "But we're overlooking something. Your agents are all unaccounted for, except for the two with you who were killed. I knew there was something I was forgetting! If all three of them were taken out, it suggests the possibility that our friends from the alternate timeline have a means of tracing warp discs. Probably by scanning for them in the same manner Search and Retrieve units conduct their sweeps."

"Which means they could have taken out the adjustment team," said Phoenix.

"Perhaps not. Drakov was going to turn you over for interrogation. An adjustment team would clearly be more valuable to them alive than dead, for the same reason. They may have taken your agents prisoner, as well.''

"Assuming they're alive," said Phoenix, "what are the chances they're still in our timeline?"

"Impossible to say," said Darkness. "If there are soldiers from the alternate timeline active in that area, they must have a base of operations somewhere. I'd guess it would be close to the confluence, which narrows the area down to the vicinity of the Khyber Pass. I'll conduct a search. Meanwhile, do you think you could infiltrate Drakov's forces without being recognized?"

"No problem, long as I don't get close enough to Drakov so he can get a good look at me. He's got thousands of men. I'll just blend in with the crowd as an Afridi."

"Good. Here's the plan then. I'll take you back there, then tach to Plus Time and warn Director Vargas. Then I'll try to find the confluence point and the enemy base of operations. I'll simply search the entire area of the Khyber Pass at light speed. I'll give you a replacement warp disc and a molecular disruptor. Try to get close to Drakov without being spotted."

"And the moment they make their move, I hit him," Phoenix said.

"Exactly."

"Okay, what are we waiting for? Let's go."

Mulvaney groaned and rolled over. "Where in the bloomin' blazes are we?"

"Sahib Finn!" cried Din.

"I'm coming, Din," Delaney said. Andre followed him down the stairs, back into the tomblike chamber.

"A fine bloody state of affairs this is," said Learoyd, sitting up slowly. "How did we get here? Wherever 'here' is."

"We're being held prisoner in an old temple high

above the Khyber Pass,'' said Finn.

''The Khyber?'' said Learoyd. ''Have we been out so long then?''

''Look 'ere, sir,'' Mulvaney said to Finn, ''what's 'appened to us? What's goin' on 'ere?''

''We've fallen into the hands of enemy soldiers,'' Finn said. ''Soldiers who are using the tribesmen for their own purposes.''

''What's their aim?'' said Learoyd.

''Apparently they're out to undermine our control of the frontier,'' Delaney said. He had to improvise. He tried to think how much he could get away with telling them.

''That one officer was American,'' Learoyd said. ''It makes no damn sense. Why would the Americans do such a thing?''

''Some of them might be Americans,'' said Delaney, ''but I don't believe it's an American unit. They weren't wearing American uniforms. They seem to be a mixed bunch. Soldiers of fortune, perhaps.''

''The Russians,'' said Learoyd. ''That must be it. They're in the pay of the Russians.''

''I shouldn't be surprised,'' said Finn. ''However, knowing that won't help us much right now.''

''What do they intend to do with us?'' Ortheris said.

''I don't know,'' said Finn. ''Question us, most likely. Find out about troop strength and the like, I should imagine.''

''Well, we've got to figure some way out of here,'' Learoyd said. ''Where do those stairs back there lead?''

''To a parapet overlooking the Khyber Pass,'' said Finn. ''Forget it. There's no way down. And the door's too heavy for us to break through.''

''We'll have to try and jump them when they come for us,'' Learoyd said. ''There's nothin' else for it. We haven't anythin' to lose.''

"I doubt they'll give us a chance," said Finn. "They know what they're doing."

"Well, we can't just sit 'ere!" said Mulvaney. "We've got to *do* something! C'mon, mates, we've been in tougher scrapes than this!"

"The best thing we can do is bide our time and wait for an opportunity," Delaney said, worried that the headstrong Mulvaney might do something foolish. "I'm in command here, and I won't have any man throwing his life away trying to be a hero. Getting ourselves killed won't solve anything."

"He's right, you know," Learoyd said. "We've got to keep our heads cool. Lieutenant, you say there's no way down off that balcony. Might there be a way *up*?"

Delaney shook his head. "We'd have to stand on each other's shoulders to reach the rocks above, and we'd never make it without climbing gear. It would be suicide."

"It could be worth a try," Learoyd said. "If one of us could make it—"

"I say we give it a go!" Mulvaney said.

"What do you say, Lieutenant?" said Learoyd. "What have we got to lose?"

"A man's life," Delaney said.

Learoyd shrugged. "That's not so very much, now is it? Let's have a look."

They went up the stairs and stood out on the windswept parapet high above the pass. Learoyd looked up. "Lord, I see what you mean," he said. "We would indeed have to stand on one another's shoulders for one of us to reach that overhangin' rock up there, and then there's no tellin' what's beyond."

Mulvaney spat into his hands and rubbed them together. "Well, who's first then?"

"I think I'll have to go," Learoyd said. "I'm the lightest."

"Sahib," said Din. "Let me. I am smallest, no? Din good climber."

"You're sure you want to try it, Din?" Learoyd said.

" 'E is the lightest," Ortheris said, "and I ain't much good with me sore arm."

"All right, Din," said Finn. "Be careful."

"Up you go, Lieutenant," said Mulvaney. He braced himself and Finn climbed up on his shoulders. Ortheris stood beside Mulvaney to brace him and Andre took the other side as they started to form a human pyramid. Finn stood up on Mulvaney's shoulders, only too aware of the yawning abyss beneath them.

"All right, Learoyd, you're next," said Finn.

Learoyd carefully climbed up, balancing himself on Mulvaney's shoulder and Ortheris's good shoulder. Slowly he stood up and placed an arm around Delaney for support.

"Don't look down," said Finn.

Learoyd, of course, looked down at the drop below them, and quickly shut his eyes. "On second thought, perhaps this wasn't such a very good idea," he said.

"You all right?" said Finn.

Learoyd swallowed hard and nodded. "Right. Next man."

"Come on, Din," said Finn.

Carefully Din climbed up Mulvaney's back, holding onto the private's burly shoulders for support.

"Come on, old son," Learoyd said, holding out his hand, "you'll make it."

Slowly, ever so slowly, so as not to upset their precarious balance, Din stood up and Ortheris groaned, gritting his teeth from the pain as Din put his weight on his bad shoulder.

"Forgive me, Sahib!"

"Never mind that," said Ortheris, "just get on up there!"

Carefully, Din climbed up to the next level of the pyramid, putting one foot on Delaney's knee. Transferring his weight slowly, he moved to sit astride Delaney's shoulders.

"Can you reach it, Din?" said Learoyd.

Din looked up and swallowed hard. "Must stand, Sahib."

"All right, then, stand. But slowly, mind!"

Moving as slowly as he could, Din placed his knees on Learoyd and Delaney's shoulders. He could see, directly below him, the dizzying drop to the bottom. The wind whipped at them and the human pyramid swayed slightly.

"Hold on there, Stanley, damn your eyes!" Learoyd shouted.

"It's me shoulder, Chris. It's killin' me."

"I'll bloody well kill you if you move again! You so much as twitch and I'll have your guts for garters!"

Muttering a prayer to himself, Din slowly stood up as Learoyd and Delaney held onto his ankles to give him some support. He didn't dare look down. The rock outcropping was directly above him. If he stretched his arms out, he could reach it.

Behind them there was the sound of the heavy bolt being drawn back and then the massive door opening. Men ran into the room. Gritting his teeth, Din pushed off Learoyd and Delaney's shoulders and jumped.

"You! Get down from—"

The pyramid collapsed. Andre, Ortheris, and Mulvaney fell to the floor of the parapet. Finn hit the surrounding wall as he went down and scrambled for a purchase. He felt Learoyd beneath him, grabbing onto his legs for dear life. The added weight almost took him over. Learoyd hung over the abyss, clinging to his legs.

"Hold on, Chris!"

"Don't you worry about me, mate," Learoyd called back. "Just *you* hold on!"

Above them Din clung to the rock, straining to pull himself up. There was no going back now. If he lost his grip, he would plummet to his death. Using every ounce of strength he had, he clawed desperately for a hold.

Several tribesmen peered over the side at Delaney and Learoyd, grinning. The officer named Martin looked down at them.

"Very cute," he said. "I ought to let you fall." He glanced back at the others, being held back at gunpoint. "You," he said, pointing to Mulvaney. "Give them a hand."

Mulvaney came forward and braced Finn while Learoyd slowly shimmied up Delaney's legs until he could reach Mulvaney's outstretched hand. Moments later they were safe.

"That was a damn fool thing to do," said Martin. He frowned and made a quick count. "Somebody's missing. The Hindu."

One of the tribesmen shouted out something and fired his rifle at the rock above them. They caught a glimpse of Din's legs disappearing out of sight atop the rock outcropping.

" 'E made it!" shouted Mulvaney. "Good ol' Din!"

Martin turned to several of the tribesmen and addressed them in Pushtu. "Get him. Bring him back alive if you can, but if you have to, shoot him."

"You bloody bastard!" roared Mulvaney, lunging at him.

The tribesmen at once shifted their aim to Mulvaney, and Learoyd leaped at them, knocking three down with his weight. Finn grappled with Martin as Andre and Ortheris took on the other tribesmen. Two men grabbed hold of Mulvaney, but he wrenched loose and one of the men fell back against the wall. His momentum carried him over the side. His scream receded in the distance.

One of the tribesmen slammed Ortheris against the wall with his rifle, and the soldier cried out from the pain in his wounded shoulder. The tribesmen struck him in the stomach with the rifle butt and was about to bring it down upon his head when Andre intervened. She had disarmed one of the tribesmen by kicking his rifle out of his grasp, then continuing the motion to launch a spinning back kick that knocked him down the stairs. She grabbed the other tribesman's rifle before he could bring it down on Ortheris's head, and kicked his legs out from under him.

Learoyd was still struggling with the men he had knocked to the floor, trying to keep them from drawing their knives, when Finn yelled out in Pushtu, "Stop or I'll kill the holy one!"

He had wrestled Martin's laser away from him and held the soldier before him, weapon to his head. The tribesmen stopped fighting.

"I was right," said Finn. "They think you're some kind of sacred demigod. That's how you've been keeping them in line, isn't it?"

Mulvaney had knocked one of the tribesmen senseless, and when Finn yelled, he had another hoisted high above his head. He stood, holding the man aloft.

"Put that man down, Mulvaney," Finn said.

"Right you are, sir!"

He dropped the tribesman over the side. His scream sent the others cowering back.

"Well, you did say to put 'im down, sir," said Mulvaney.

"There's no way you're going to get out of here," said Martin. "Using me as a hostage might work with these superstitious Ghazis, but my men will never fall for it. They'll shoot us both."

"Then we'll go together, won't we?" said Finn. "Learoyd, Ortheris, Andre, get their weapons. And shut that door."

Moments later they had the Ghazis tied up and

gagged with strips torn from a couple of their robes.
The other robes were saved for use as disguises.

"All right," said Finn, covering Martin. "We're
going out of here the same way you came in. I'll be right
behind you."

Martin shook his head. "I'm not going anywhere."

Mulvaney came up behind him and twisted his arm up
behind his back. Martin gasped with pain. "You'll do as
the lieutenant says, mate, or I'll break yer bloody arm
and then I'll start on somethin' else."

With Mulvaney keeping a firm grasp on Martin's
arm, they moved out into the corridor. "Which way?"
Mulvaney said.

"Go to hell," said Martin.

Mulvaney forced his arm up higher, and Martin cried
out.

"Enough of that," said Finn. "I remember the way.
We go left."

Frog-marching Martin before them, they headed
toward the main chamber. When they reached the corridor that led to it, Delaney had them stop.

"You three go on," he said.

"What do you mean, go on?" Learoyd said. "What
about you?"

"We'll follow you. It'll attract less attention if we
don't go out as a large group. Whatever happens, *don't
turn back*. You understand? That's an order."

"Right. Miss Cross, you come with us. Mulvaney'll
stay behind and follow with the lieutenant."

"No. You go ahead. I'm staying with Finn."

"Don't let's argue about it," said Learoyd. "Come
on, now, we haven't got much time."

"I said I'm staying. I can take care of myself, Chris.
Now go. Hurry."

Learoyd shook his head. "I swear, you're the most
stubborn woman I ever laid eyes on, but you can handle

yourself in a pinch, I'll grant you that. For God's sake, be careful. Off now, lads.''

Finn let them get a good start, then he forced Martin up against the wall. "All right, where'd you put our warp discs?"

Martin smiled. "Why don't you guess?"

"Okay, we'll take a little walk and look for them."

Martin grinned. "Suit yourselves."

Keeping him in front of them, they headed back toward the room where they had spoken with the twin Priest. They passed a number of tribesmen on their way, but Martin didn't try anything, and they kept their heads down to keep from being recognized.

"So far, so good," said Andre.

"So far it's too easy," Finn said.

"You complaining?"

"No, but where are all the soldiers we saw before?"

"I don't much care, to tell you the truth," said Andre. "Long as they're not here."

They reached the room they were seeking and shoved Martin inside ahead of them. There was no one there. Finn pushed Martin into a chair and gave Andre the laser to cover him while he searched the room.

"What's going on, Martin?" he said. "Where is everyone?"

"Maybe they all went on leave," said Martin.

"We're not going to get anything out of him," said Andre. "He's no different from our Martin in that respect."

"I'll take that as a compliment," said the soldier from the alternate timeline.

"Shut up," said Delaney, searching the gear in the storage cabinets at the far end of the room. "Where the hell did they put them?"

"Are these what you're looking for?"

A pair of warp discs landed on the table in front of

Martin. Finn spun around. Captain Bryant stood in the entrance with four soldiers behind him. He had a laser trained on Finn. "Go ahead," he said, with a half smile. "Do you feel lucky?"

Gunga Din perched precariously on a rocky ledge above the balcony. He had managed to climb perhaps twenty feet. To his left, about fifty feet away, was a large hollow in the rock wall where part of the temple stood, surrounded by the cliffs. He could see the walled enclosure of an open space, a large balcony with several carved statues of Kali between pillars supporting the rock overhead, and farther in, another part of the temple. A number of Ghazis had come out onto that balcony and shot at him with their jezails, but he scuttled around to the far side of the small ledge, out of their line of fire. They kept shooting for a short while, laughing, but soon wearied of the game and went away. They could not get at him, but neither could he go anywhere. There was no place left to go. He could not climb any higher, there was no place that would afford him adequate hand or footholds to the right or to the left, and he could not go back down. He was trapped.

He sat there, miserable, shivering from the wind which lashed at him. He had no idea what to do. There was nothing he could do. He had failed. The soldiers had counted on him, and he had failed. He would sit on that ledge, unable to go anywhere, until he became weak or desperate and could bear it no longer, and then he would die. He could see no point to prolonging the inevitable. He closed his eyes and muttered a brief prayer to Brahma the Creator, giving thanks for the life he had led and asking his blessings in the next one. Then he said a prayer to Vishnu the Preserver, to redeem the karma of his soul as the sun redeems the earth from darkness. He said a prayer to Shiva the Destroyer, asking that the end be swift, and at the last, he prayed to the avatar of Vishnu, the hero-god Krishna, asking that his karma lead him to a better existence in the next life. Then he raised his battered bugle to his lips, determined to die not as the regimental *bhisti* he had been, but as the bugler he dreamed of being. He shut his eyes and inhaled deeply, preparing to sound Retreat.

"What in heaven's name are you doing?"

Din jerked so forcibly he almost fell off the ledge. Just before he lost his balance completely, a hand reached out to steady him. He looked up, wide-eyed, at the tall dark figure standing on the ledge beside him. He was dressed entirely in black. The coal-black eyes seemed to burn into him.

Din shut his eyes. Shiva! He had to be dead. The Destroyer had come to escort his soul to the next plane. He bent his head down low, touching the rock at Shiva's feet and praying out loud, praising the Destroyer.

"Stop that! I can't understand a word. Can't you speak English?"

Din stopped praying. *English?* The great god Shiva wanted him to speak in English? Come to think of it, the great god Shiva had spoken to *him* in English. Perhaps it was because he was wearing the English khaki uniform and served as a regimental *bhisti*. Perhaps that was now the language of his soul. Who was he to question Shiva?

"Oh, Mahadeva!" Din said, keeping his face pressed close to the rock. "Oh, great god! You who are Great Destroyer; you whose presence is felt in falling of a leaf; you who are bringer of swift and terrible death; you who—"

"I'll bring you a clout on the head if you don't stop spouting that nonsense," said Darkness. "Who are you? What are you doing up here?"

"Your humble and worthless servant, Gunga Din, oh, Mahadeva!"

"Well, fine. That settles who you are. Now what are you doing here? How the devil did you get up here anyway? Look at me."

Din slowly raised his face up to stare in terror at the avatar. Something was wrong. Perhaps he wasn't dead yet after all.

"Din try to escape, help soldiers, O Great One."

"Soldiers? What soldiers?"

"The Sahibs Finn, Learoyd, O'tris, and Mulvaney. And the Memsahib Cross, O Great One."

"Where are they?"

"In temple, Mahadeva. In greatest danger. Din try to escape, try to help—"

"And you got stuck up here, I see," said Darkness. "Well, you've got a lot of nerve, I'll give you that. I suppose we'd better get you out of this mess. Here, give me your hand."

This, then, was the moment, Din thought. Shiva would now lead him into the next life. He shut his eyes and held out a shaking hand to Darkness. He felt himself pulled forward, and kept his eyes tightly shut, not wanting to see the terrifying drop, not wanting to see the end, afraid to catch glimpses of things in the next world that mortal eyes were never meant to see.

"Open your eyes."

Din opened his eyes. He was on the parapet from where the Ghazis had shot at him, not fifty feet from where he had perched upon the ledge. He looked down at himself and saw that he was still unchanged. His soul had not been reincarnated into some other form of life, into an insect or an animal or a bird, nor had it been reincarnated into the body of a high-caste infant; it had been reincarnated back into himself, Gunga Din, unchanged, still in his khakis.

"What are you staring at? Go on. You're safe. You're on your own now. I've got things to do."

Darkness disappeared.

Gunga Din was mystified. How could this be? Had he not died? He *must* have died! He had seen the great god Shiva, the Destroyer! He had felt himself falling forward, pulled by the hand of Shiva into the yawning void. He felt himself. He felt solid. He felt the same way he always had. There could only be one explanation. It was not the destiny of his soul to be reincarnated into another form of life. He had not acquired enough good karma. His karma was to be a regimental *bhisti* until he earned the right to be reborn into a higher plane. Shiva had given him another opportunity to prove himself worthy. Din swelled with pride at the thought. He would not fail this time.

10

Andre had her laser pointed at Martin. Bryant had his pointing at Finn. He smiled. "Well, it seems we have a standoff. You kill Martin, I kill Delaney. And then where will that leave us? You might be quick enough to try a shot at me, but with four other weapons pointed at you, I doubt you'd make it."

"Either way, Martin dies," said Andre.

"Well, that would be regrettable," said Bryant, "but it wouldn't change the outcome. I'm prepared to lose Martin if I must. If you're determined to die and you want to take at least one man with you, go ahead and shoot. Personally, I think it would be pointless."

Andre hesitated.

"He's right, Andre," said Finn. "They've got us."

"Damn," said Andre. She lowered her laser and Martin took it from her grasp.

He chuckled, but the sound froze in his throat when he saw Bryant and the others suddenly enveloped in the blue mist of Cherenkov radiation. A second later all five men were gone, their atoms disintegrated. Darkness lowered the molecular disruptor.

Martin yelled and fired at him point-blank, but he was no longer there.

"Try over here," said Darkness from the other side of the room.

Martin fired again, but the target had disappeared.

"Behind you."

Martin spun around and Andre and Finn both dropped to the floor as he fired wildly all around the room, vainly trying to keep up with a target that moved faster than the speed of light.

"Hi," said Darkness, manifesting directly in front of Martin, about three inches away. Martin screamed and leaped back, but Darkness was gone again. His eyes staring madly all about the room, Martin kept jerking to the left and to the right, spinning around, trying to find something to shoot at. A fist materialized out of thin air and connected with his jaw. Martin collapsed to the floor, unconscious.

Darkness reappeared seated in one of the chairs. "God, I'm exhausted."

Finn and Andre both got up off the floor. "Having fun?" Delaney said.

Darkness stared at him. "You're welcome," he said. "I pull your butts out of the fire again and you begrudge me even some minor amusement. You're an ungrateful man, Delaney."

"I'd have been a damn sight more ungrateful if one of those wild shots had hit me," Finn said. "I'm glad to see you, Doctor. We could sure use some help. How'd you find us?"

"Peculiar little chap named Gunga Din told me you were here," said Darkness. "I was looking for the confluence when I spotted him sitting on a ledge out there, looking unutterably morose.''

"God, we've got to get him down from there!" said Andre.

"No, no, he's all right," said Darkness. "He's running about somewhere. The important thing right now is to do something about these characters. I left that one alive to tell me where to find the confluence. I know it's around here somewhere, but I can't seem to pinpoint it."

"So you know all about it then?" said Finn.

"Of course I know all about it, you cretin. What do you think we're talking about? Vargas has already been warned, and I expect he's gotten on to Colonel Forrester. However, there's a certain question of timing involved, and a few other minor problems. But before I do anything else, I need to find the confluence point."

"We can help you there," said Andre. "It's right below us. We spotted several of them coming through with jet-paks. There's a narrow section of the pass down there, directly below this temple, where the walls jut out like two giant pillars. The confluence point is there."

"Well, then it was fortunate for me I saw that little fellow sitting on the ledge," said Darkness. "I was about to go right through there. I haven't yet perfected a means of measuring for inertial surge. That's the key, you understand. The phenomenon is truly fascinating. What we have here is—"

"Doc," said Finn, "I don't mean to sound rude, but we can get into temporal physics some other time, okay? You said there were problems. What problems?"

"Oh, well, it's a question of timing, partly. It appears as if their plan is to support Sayyid Akbar in his fight against the Tirah Expeditionary Force."

"I knew it!" Andre said. "That must be where the others have gone, to check on the progress of the force.

With their help, Sayyid Akbar will be able to set up an ambush, and then they'll bring their own troops in to do the mopping up.''

"It's a bit more complex than that, I'm afraid," said Darkness. "Sayyid Akbar is none other than our old friend, Nikolai Drakov."

"What?" said Andre.

"He must have stumbled through a confluence somehow," said Darkness, "or perhaps created one by actions of his own. He fell into their hands and now they're using him to control the Ghazis."

Delaney strapped on his warp disc. "I'm getting really tired of tripping over Drakov at every turn," he said. "This time he's not getting away."

"This time he's not a great priority," said Darkness.

A tribesman came through the door. Before either Finn or Andre had a chance to move, the tribesman had collapsed to the floor as if felled by an unseen hand.

"Where was I?" Darkness said, apparently not having moved from his chair. "Oh, yes, Drakov. Forget about Drakov for the moment. There's something much more important. When I tached to Plus Time and briefed Vargas about the situation, I discovered they had arrested one of the programmers in the archives section of TAC-HQ. He was caught tampering with the implant education and mission program files. A clear-cut case of sabotage. The historians were called in to run a scan check on the files, and they discovered a number of them had been tampered with. They ran a cross-check on the subknowledge of various adjustment personnel and confirmed that the sabotage goes back a number of years. I think you'll find one of the discoveries made by the historians significant. All data pertaining to Winston Spenser Churchill had been altered. He was entirely erased from all the archive files."

"That explains it!" Andre said. "We encountered Churchill while we were with the Malakand field force, but only Lucas knew who he was. Or rather, what he would become. Neither Finn nor I knew he would become prime minister of Great Britain, because there was nothing about him in our subknowledge or in the mission programming. Lucas couldn't understand it. An omission like that seemed inconceivable, but then he realized that he didn't know about Churchill through *his* subknowledge either. He remembered reading about him."

"He gave his life to save Churchill's," Finn said.

"Yes, I know," said Darkness. "I'm sorry."

"We thought the incongruity had something to do with Churchill being the focus of a disruption, but that wasn't it. It was sabotage. Christ, it's all starting to fit together now. They must have discovered a confluence in Plus Time. Either that, or used the confluence back here to get someone through and clock ahead to the 27th century. They infiltrated someone into the archives section with instructions to delete all programming having to do with certain key historical individuals—*targeted* individuals. But they didn't count on history books. Only a small group of dedicated scholars and antiquarians read books anymore. Everyone else uses information retrieval systems. They couldn't have known one of the commandos sent back on the adjustment was a history fanatic. Lucas was a collector of old history books, specializing in the 18th, 19th, and 20th centuries."

"There's an anomaly right there," said Andre. "It's one example of how their timeline differs from ours. Their Lucas Priest can't be an historian, otherwise he would have suspected that ours might be."

"*Their* Lucas Priest?" said Darkness.

"An identical twin from the alternate timeline," said Delaney. "It's scary. He's the one in command of their advance force."

"Incredible," said Darkness. "The Fate Factor never ceases to amaze me. But you realize what all this means. The strike against the Tirah Expeditionary Force is only part of their overall plan. They're out to create a massive historical disruption in the hope that it will force the two timelines apart and eliminate the confluence effect that endangers them both. What they don't realize is that there's every possibility a time stream split could only make matters worse by compounding the problem. It could result in *three* timelines experiencing a confluence effect. In fact, I believe the odds favor that possibility. Once such an effect was under way, it could be impossible to stop it. We'd wind up with four timelines, then five, then six, leading to God only knows what. However, since they apparently don't know that, they're out to create a timestream split, and this scenario offers them an outstanding opportunity. Defeat of the Tirah Expeditionary Force could end British control of the frontier and drastically alter the picture in this part of the world. And assassinating Winston Churchill in the same scenario would not only further disrupt history in this time period, but it would disrupt it in the early 20th century as well. It could lead to not one, but *two* timestream splits."

"That's why they sabotaged the archives," Finn said in a low voice. "They didn't want an adjustment team to know that Churchill was a key historical figure and concentrate on covering him. We left him on the march to Chakdarra. Christ, he's wide open."

"And Priest and some of his men are gone," said Andre.

"There's not a moment to lose," said Darkness. "You must find Churchill. I'll help you if I can, but I need to keep track of their movements against the British Expeditionary Force, as well as maintain a watch on the confluence point. I need to recuperate, and besides, I can only be in two places at the same time."

"We'll find Churchill, Doc. You've got enough on your hands."

"Here, take this," said Darkness, handing Finn the disruptor. "Between that and the laser, you should have adequate firepower. Don't hesitate to use it."

"Count on it."

"Good luck."

"And good luck to you, Doctor," said Andre. They programmed their warp discs and clocked out.

"Somethin's gone wrong," Learoyd said. "They haven't come out."

"I knew we shouldn't 'ave left 'em," said Mulvaney. "Bloody green subaltern's goin' to get 'imself killed for sure."

"We've got to go back," said Learoyd.

"Go back?" said Ortheris. "Are you out o' your mind?"

Learoyd turned on him angrily. "What the hell do you want to do, Stanley? Leave them there? Fine! You can turn tail and tuck it up between your legs while you're about it! Go back to Peshawar and warn the troops. I suppose someone's got to do it. But I'm not walkin' out on Finn and Andre, no sir, not Chris Learoyd! I'm not one to leave friends in a lurch. You with me, Mulvaney?"

"I never was much for sneakin' about an' keeping me 'ead down," said Mulvaney. "I say we go back an' give those sods what for!"

"Well, if we're goin' to kill ourselves, we might as well do it together," said Ortheris. "You're right, mate, we can't just leave 'em. What's the plan then?"

"They'll never expect us to return, that's for certain," Learoyd said. "That should work in our favor. We sneak back in the same way we got out, posin' as Ghazis. Mulvaney, fix your puggaree. I can see your red hair stickin' out."

Mulvaney adjusted his turban.

"Right. Let's go."

Walking boldly and purposefully, they headed back toward the temple. They passed the sentries without any trouble and went up the stone stairs into the columned entryway. They were greeted by several tribesmen inside, and Learoyd replied in Pushtu, keeping his answers brief and guttural for fear of betraying an accent. They were almost to the far end of the main chamber when a voice cried out, echoing in the stone hall, "On your knees! On your knees before the Light of Islam!"

They turned around and saw a man standing in the center of the chamber, flanked by four guards. He was tall and muscular, dressed entirely in black with loose-fitting trousers, a flowing, long-sleeved shirt, high black boots, and a vest intricately embroidered in gold. He wore a black turban fastened with a giant ruby clasp. The tribesmen in the chamber immediately dropped to all fours, pressing their heads to the floor. The three soldiers did likewise.

"Where the devil did *they* come from?" whispered Ortheris. "They weren't behind us, were they?"

"Did you hear what he said?" Learoyd whispered. "The Light of Islam. That's none other than Sayyid Akbar himself."

"Now that's what I call a stroke o' luck," Mulvaney said. "We can shoot the blighter where 'e stands an' end this jehad once an' for all."

"Don't be a fool," Learoyd hissed. "And keep your damn voice down! You'll give us away."

Drakov ignored the kneeling tribesmen and walked

quickly across the chamber, heading for the innermost part of the temple with his guard accompanying him.

"Let's follow them," Learoyd whispered, "but not too close. Watch yourselves."

They followed Drakov and his guards down the long corridor which ran to the left of the giant obsidian statue of Kali. Drakov's guards stopped outside one of the chambers and took up posts by the entrance while Drakov went inside.

"We can't pass this up," Mulvaney whispered as they approached. "There's only four of 'em. We can slit their throats with these 'ere knives an' then do in that miserable fakir. We might never get another chance, Chris."

"I said *no*," Learoyd whispered. "We've got to find Finn and Andre first. We're the only chance they've got."

They had to pass the guards on their way to the cell where they were being kept before. They kept their heads down and grunted as they went by.

"You three!" Drakov called out behind them.

They stopped.

"Bloody 'Ell!" whispered Ortheris.

"Turn and face me when I speak to you!" said Drakov.

They turned slowly, keeping their heads down, as if with great humility.

"Where are the warriors of the host of heaven?"

"What the devil is 'e talkin' about?" whispered Mulvaney.

"How the hell should I know?" Learoyd whispered back. Then, with his head still bowed, he replied in Pushtu, "I do not know, Your Holiness."

Drakov stood silent for a moment, thinking. "I am told there are British soldiers being held prisoner here. Take me to them."

"Well, what do you know?" whispered Mulvaney. "We're goin' to get our chance at Sayyid bloody Akbar, after all."

Learoyd elbowed him in the ribs. "This way, Your Holiness," he said, bowing low and pointing out the way.

"Lead on," said Drakov.

"Steady, lads," whispered Learoyd. "Steady now."

They walked ahead of Drakov and his guards, heading toward the cell they had recently escaped from. They paused at the door. Drakov stopped in front of it.

"This door is unbolted! What is the meaning of this?" He opened it. "There's no one inside! Where are the prisoners?" He reached out and jerked Mulvaney's head up. "You're not—"

Mulvaney slammed a hard right into his stomach and pushed him into the cell. Learoyd plunged his knife deep into the abdomen of one of the guards while Ortheris kicked another in the groin with all his might and stuck his knife into the other's chest. Learoyd wrestled briefly with the fourth guard, his hand clamped over his mouth, then slashed his blade across his throat. Ortheris disposed of the one remaining guard, who was on the floor, clutching at his vitals. They quickly dragged the corpses into the cell and shut the door.

Learoyd had Drakov backed up against the stone wall, the point of his Khyber knife against his throat.

"Well, well," said Mulvaney, grinning. "Look what we've got 'ere!"

He had lost his turban in the scuffle, and Drakov stared at him, then at the others. "Who are you men?"

"You speak English!" said Ortheris, not so much surprised to hear a Pathan speaking it as he was to hear it spoken so well, without an accent.

"You're the soldiers," Drakov said. "I commend you on your resourcefulness. Where are the others who were being held with you, a man and a woman?"

"Look at this, will you?" Ortheris said. "A knife at 'is throat an' 'e's demandin' answers like a bleedin' rajah!"

"That's just what we're here to find out, Your Holiness," Learoyd said.

"Chris, watch 'is 'ands!" cried Mulvaney.

Learoyd quickly batted Drakov's right hand away from his left wrist. It looked as if he had been reaching for a dagger hidden up his sleeve. Mulvaney quickly stepped up and checked.

"What's this?" he said, examining the warp disc on Drakov's wrist. He pulled at it, trying to figure out how to take it off, and managed to yank it loose.

"What is it?" said Learoyd.

"Looks like some sort o' bracelet," said Mulvaney.

"Be careful with it," said Learoyd. "These devils can be tricky. It might have some sort of poisoned needle in it or the like."

Mulvaney flung it away from him and it landed in the far corner of the room. "Right," he said. "Let's finish 'im off."

"Don't be too hasty," Drakov said. "I'm your best chance of finding your friends. As long as I'm alive, you remain alive. If you harm me, they'll cut you to pieces."

"I'm afraid you're right," Learoyd said. "Where'd you learn to speak English so well?"

Drakov smiled. "You would not belive me if I told you."

"I say we kill 'im an' 'ave done with it!" Mulvaney said.

"No, let's not be rash," Learoyd said. "He has a point. If we kill him now, we may never get through this alive. He's our ticket out of here. And he can get us safe passage to Peshawar. Wouldn't that be something, us ridin' in with Sayyid Akbar himself? We'd be heroes."

"Live heroes are generally preferable over dead ones," Drakov said.

"You keep shut," Learoyd said. "Mulvaney, take him. He's a big one, but he won't break away from you. Get on, you."

They pushed him out into the corridor. It was filled with heavily armed tribesmen.

"Blast!" Learoyd said.

"Now aren't you glad you didn't kill me?" Drakov said, smiling.

"Tell them to back away!"

"You tell them. You speak the language well enough."

"I want it comin' from you." Learoyd jabbed him with the knife. *"Now."*

Drakov called out to the tribesmen to back away. They did so, slowly, keeping their weapons ready.

"Now ask them where they've got the prisoners."

Drakov called out to the tribesmen again. There was a brief silence, then one of the men answered.

"There are no prisoners, Your Holiness. There are only those with you. The others have escaped."

"Escaped?" said Ortheris.

"They're lyin'," said Mulvaney. "We never saw 'em come out."

"Why don't you search the other chambers then?" said Drakov. "I'm in no great hurry to go anywhere. I'll wait."

"I don't like this," Ortheris said. "This chap's actin' too cocksure of 'imself."

"I have nothing to lose," said Drakov. "You don't dare risk harming me. And as for getting me to Peshawar, you're dreaming. If you think about it, you'll see how hopeless your position is."

"We'll see about that," Learoyd said. "Come on."

They proceeded farther down the hall to check the

other chambers. Mulvaney kept a firm grip on Drakov while Learoyd and Ortheris quickly checked the rooms. Each one they came to was empty. There was no sign of Finn and Andre. The tribesmen followed, keeping their distance, alert for any opportunity to attack and rescue their holy man. Among them, his khakis hidden by a long white robe, was Gunga Din.

11

The British camp was below them, on the plain before the Bedmanai Pass. It was Mohmand territory, the land of the savage tribesmen of the Mamund Valley. After the relief of Chakdarra, Blood had pressed on to put down the revolt of the Mohmands, who though they had been deserted by Sadullah, nevertheless had no shortage of holy men to spur them on in their jehad. The entire frontier situation was unstable, from Chitral to the Khyber Pass. The fever of jehad had spread like a disease, infecting all those tribes except those already pacified by force of arms.

General Blood knew he could not fail to put down the rebellion. It was not enough to defeat Sadullah at the Malakand Pass, nor was it enough to rescue the garrison at Chakdarra. He needed to put down each and every tribe, thwart each and every holy man who incited the mountain people to revolt. Those tribes that had been defeated by him, those khans who had been forced to make peace along his line of march, would remain subjugated only so long as he did not fail. One defeat, one withdrawal, one serious setback, or one recalcitrant tribe not met on its own ground would be interpreted as a sign of weakness, and those khans who had so humbly and respectfully agreed to terms would immediately rise up again, like the embers of a campfire not properly doused would soon erupt in flame.

Finn and Andre stood upon a rise overlooking the British camp. They knew from history that this was one of the most difficult moments in Blood's campaign. Before him was the Bedmanai Pass, held by the Ghazi followers of Hadda Mullah. Behind him was ground broken by ravines and nullahs, across which retreat would be extremely difficult. He had only one brigade with him. The 2nd Brigade, which had been meant to rendezvous here with him, was still engaged in fighting in the Mamund Valley, twelve miles away. The 1st Brigade was stuck with transport problems on the Panjkora River. A relief division was still miles away, struggling to get through difficult and hostile country. Blood was squarely in the middle at Nawagai.

Heliograph communications under such conditions were difficult, as was the local khan, who was "loyal" to the British only while Blood remained encamped upon his doorstep. If he went to reinforce the 2nd Brigade, the khan of Nawagai would turn against him and the Hadda Mullah's Ghazis would pour down out of the Bedmanai Pass to harass his rear. The entire region would be out of control. Blood's brigade was the only thing between the Hadda Mullah's Ghazis and the tribesmen in the Mamund. If they were to unite, his situation, and that of the British in the northern sector of the frontier, would almost certainly be hopeless.

"He's down there somewhere," Finn said, "a young cavalry officer on leave from his regiment and having a high old time. Can you beat that? Most soldiers go on leave so they can see their loved ones or have a party

somewhere. This one goes so he can see a war. It's not
enough he's faced with thousands of berserkers with
knives and swords and rifles, now he's got a hit squad
from a parallel future on his tail. 'How was your leave,
soldier?' 'Oh, not so bad, sir. Bit of a dustup with
several thousand savages; some difficulty crossing
rugged terrain while being harassed by snipers night and
day; a few assassins from an alternate universe gave us a
rough time for a while, but otherwise, routine, sir. Just
routine.' What was that line about mad dogs and
Englishmen?"

"You're tense," said Andre. "You always babble in-
coherently when you get tense."

Delaney snorted. "You're feeling relaxed and mel-
low, I suppose?"

"Sure. I'm fine now. When this is over, I'm going to
have a nervous breakdown. I hope to hell you've read
the situation right."

"I hope to hell I have too," said Finn. "If I was going
to do what they're planning, this would be the perfect
opportunity. This was a turning point in Blood's campaign. If he failed here, the whole northern frontier
would have gone up, and the Tirah Expeditionary Force
would have been nowhere near enough to pacify the
region. With Blood putting down the uprisings in the
north, all Lockhart had to worry about were the tribes
in the southern sector. This scenario would give them
the perfect chance to kill two birds with one stone.
Assassinate Churchill and sabotage Blood's drive
against the Bedmanai Pass. Add that to the strike
against the Tirah force in the Khyber and you've got a
massive temporal disruption on several counts, with at
least one timestream split, guaranteed."

"How do you think they'll go about it?" Andre said.

"If I was them, I'd wait for the battle," Finn said.

"It would be easier for them to kill Churchill in all the confusion."

"You don't think they're down there already, do you?"

"I doubt it. It would be difficult to infiltrate a brigade that's been together as long as this one has. Most of the men would know each other, and strangers would be spotted pretty quickly. And infiltrating the tribesmen would make it that much harder for them to get close to Churchill. Easier when you're on the same side. No, they'll wait for all hell to break loose when the brigade goes up against the Ghazis. My guess is they're out here somewhere in the dark, just like we are. Waiting."

"Or looking for us," said Andre. "If they can scan for warp discs, then they know we're here."

"I'm betting against it," Finn said. "They have no reason to carry scanning equipment with them on this trip. They want to travel light. And as far as they know, we're still back in that cell inside the temple, being interrogated by Bryant and the others in the party."

"Unless one of them's gone back to check in," she said. "Any way you look at it, we're taking a big gamble."

"True," said Finn, grinning at her, "but you're taking it with an Irishman. That's as near to a sure thing as you can get."

"I'd still feel better if we had the entire First Division with us," Andre said. "I'm also worried about Mulvaney, Ortheris, and Learoyd."

"I know," said Finn. "I hope they weren't foolish enough to go back when they saw we didn't come out."

"They're just the type who would," said Andre.

Finn nodded. "Much as I hate to say it, we can't afford to worry about them now. Their lives aren't as important as Churchill's. We have to take care of the hit squad first. Then we can go back for them."

"Assuming we're still alive."

"We will be. I'm not quite ready to retire yet. We need to get close to Churchill in a hurry when things start happening," said Finn. "I don't like trying to clock into the middle of a battle and looking for him while everybody's shooting at each other."

"You're right. I think we should go down there," Andre said.

"How do we explain our presence? We were sent back to Peshawar from Malakand, remember?"

"True, but what if we never got there?"

"Okay, what are you thinking?"

"Listen to this and tell me if it sounds plausible. We started out towards Peshawar, but ran into enemy tribesmen on the way. We ran, but we couldn't get through. We became separated from the others when my horse was shot out from under me. You turned back to help me, and we were cut off. We managed to escape and we followed the regiment, keeping to concealment as much as possible. Your horse went lame several miles away from here and we had to chance going the rest of the way on foot. We arrive at the brigade camp looking very tired, and relieved as all hell to get through with our skins intact. What do you think?"

"Not bad," said Finn. "I don't think they'll have any reason to question the story. We already look pretty bedraggled, but it'll help if we mess our clothes up a bit more. It'll get us back into the camp, and we'll be able to keep close to Churchill. I like it. You'd better carry the disruptor. We can tear up these robes a bit and rig up a way to tie it to your thigh. It might be difficult to conceal on me, and I don't think anyone will go looking up your dress. These are Englishmen, after all."

"Too bad," she said, smiling. "I was going to suggest

one way to keep close to Churchill tonight."

Delaney stared at her.

"Just kidding."

"With you, sometimes it's hard to tell."

They made their preparations and then started down toward the camp. "Be careful," said Finn. "We don't want to get shot by the pickets."

When they were a short distance from the camp, Finn spotted the picket line. At almost the same time an alert soldier spotted him. A shot sent them both sprawling face down in the dirt.

"Hold your fire!" Finn shouted.

The astonished soldier challenged them, and when Finn replied, told them to come forward.

"All right, here goes," said Finn. "Cross your fingers. We may be able to pull this off yet."

"You won't find your friends," said Drakov.

"What 'ave you done with 'em?" Mulvaney said, tightening his grip.

"Finn Delaney and Andre Cross have made good their escape," said Drakov.

"How did you know their names?" Learoyd said.

"There is more involved here than you could imagine," Drakov said. "Far more than I can allow you to interfere with. They understood how much was at stake, and they could not afford to concern themselves with you. Neither can I."

He broke Mulvaney's grip easily and threw him into Ortheris. Learoyd lunged at him with the knife, but Drakov was quicker. He blocked the thrust, turned Learoyd's wrist, jerked him off balance, and chopped him to the ground. The Ghazis quickly closed in and the soldiers were taken.

"Now that I'm satisfied you're no more than what you appeared to be, I can safely dismiss you from my mind," said Drakov. "Unfortunately for you, I can't let you go. You'd warn the Tirah force and upset my plans."

"Don't you worry, mate," Mulvaney said. "We'll upset more than yer plans yet."

"Brash talk," said Drakov, "and utterly pointless." He opened the door to the cell and went inside to pick up the warp disc Mulvaney had tossed into a corner. He smiled as he came out. "If you had known what this was, you would not have treated it so casually. But then, you'll never know. I have only one question for you. What became of the soldiers who were holding you here?"

"I haven't the foggiest notion," said Learoyd. "If they had any sense, they went back to wherever it was they came from. It'll take more than a few Ghazis and a handful of mercenaries to stop the Royal Indian Army, I can tell you that."

"You may be right," said Drakov. "It will take more. And there will *be* more. Meanwhile I have wasted enough time with you."

"Then kill us and have done with it, you swine," said Learoyd.

"Doubtless my friends would dearly love to slice you into ribbons," Drakov said, "but I am not a barbarian and I see no point to having you killed. And you may be of some value to me later, one never knows. I will leave instructions for them to keep you alive."

"How bloody gracious of you," Ortheris said.

"I cannot promise more than that. After all, the British are my enemy, and I do not wish to appear *too* gracious. These cutthroats may decide to have some sport with you. Keep a stiff upper lip." He smiled. "After all, I could have had you sentenced to the Death of a Thousand Cuts. Are you familiar with that quaint custom? The victim is tied down and slowly sliced with knives.

Then thorns are pushed into the wounds as they're sliced open. And that's only one of the more creative amusements these people indulge in from time to time. We'll see each other again before too long. And then you'll have an opportunity to show me what soldiers in the Royal Indian Army are made of. Lock them up.''

Drakov watched as they were thrown into the cell, then turned and headed back toward the main chamber. He was convinced that the three soldiers posed no threat, but he was uneasy. At first he had suspected that they might be time commandos, but he never would have broken away from them so easily if they were. Martial arts worked well on 19th century British soldiers. With commandos from the 27th century, it would have been another matter entirely.

It had sent a thrill through him when he learned that the troops from the alternate universe, the commandos of the Special Operations Group, had captured Andre Cross and Finn Delaney. It was all coming to a head once more, and perhaps this time it would happen. He had failed to bring about the ultimate temporal disaster twice before. Both times Delaney, Priest, and Cross had thwarted him. This time he felt sure he would succeed. This time it would not be an army of cutthroats and killers recruited from periods throughout time, as his pirates had been, but an army of highly trained commandos from an alternate timeline, people who were the match of his father's cursed First Division.

Drakov was insane. Perhaps it had begun from childhood, when his Russian Gypsy mother tried to explain to him how he had been born, but Vanna Drakova herself had not even fully understood it. Whatever she told her son about Moses Forrester, a father from the future —a man who had been lost and badly broken, whose life she had saved and with whom she had fallen in love —whatever strange version of the story she might have told him had only served to terrify the boy.

He could not comprehend how it was possible for a father to sire a son hundreds of years before his own birth. So his highly imaginative mind, already influenced by his mother's Gypsy superstitions, led him to believe that he was born of some sort of supernatural union—a demon issue. This belief was only reinforced when he discovered that he did not sicken and that he healed from wounds with astonishing rapidity. It was reinforced further still as he got older and found that he did not age—or that he aged at a rate far slower than was normal. He did not know about such things as chronoplates or warp discs or antiagathic drug treatments until much later, but the seed of insanity was planted, nurtured by a hate for his father, who had left his mother alone and unprotected to die a violent death.

The seed of madness sprouted and began to grow when, as an adult in England, he met Sophia Falco, one of the leaders of a terrorist group known as the Time-keepers. When she learned the truth of his background, she used him to get back at Forrester. She seduced him, took him to the future with her, and obtained a black market cybernetic implant for him which, when programmed, gave him an education equal to that of a soldier in the First Division of the 27th century. And then, having fed his hate, she set the son against the father. She had failed and it resulted in her death, but she had not failed completely.

Forrester had never fully recovered from his guilt over what his son had come to, and Nikolai Drakov never understood why, at the crucial moment when he had his father at his mercy, he was unable to kill him. It had been to much. Too many things had happened to further unhinge an already unstable mind.

He escaped and formed the Time Pirates, composed of bloodthirsty mercenary soldiers from every period of time imaginable. Determined to strike back at his father and at the entire system that gave birth to him, he took upon himself the mantle of fate's avatar. He stole a Soviet nuclear submarine and planned to use its missiles to fragment the timestream. His father's commandos beat him once again, aided by the turncoat, Martingale. But they had not defeated him completely.

The consequences of that last great battle, Drakov was convinced, had brought about the confluence effect between two timelines. And he had been granted yet another opportunity. He would split the timeline, shatter it if possible into a thousand different timestreams, and in one of them, he knew, he would finally find peace. In his moments of lucidity, which came fewer and further between, he subsided into deep depression, an unutterable melancholy which made him weep for his mother and long for the normal life that might have been. At such moments he was tempted to escape, to find some tranquil period in time where he could forget it all and live out his extended lifespan in peace. But he was never able to escape from his worst enemy—himself.

The traitor Martingale had gotten away, but Drakov felt confident he would return. His father's people now knew what was being planned, and they would retaliate. So much the better. The more chaos introduced into the scenario, the greater the chance of further disrupting history. He thought the commandos had been captured, and since there had been no report of Priest, he thought one of the other prisoners might have been him. He wondered what Lucas Priest's reaction would have been when he was confronted by his twin. Now all three of them were unaccounted for. That bothered him. They were too damn resourceful, those three. And too damn lucky.

They would know about him being present on the

scene now. He counted on them coming after him. It
was one of the things he had tried to impress upon the
soldiers from the alternate timeline—their plan had to
be a multileveled one with fallback positions. The commandos had never failed in an historical adjustment,
and these three were the best of the lot. This time not
even they would be able to stop it. They might stop one
facet of the plan, but they would never stop the others.
The moment the assassination of Winston Churchill was
accomplished, and the moment the Tirah Expeditionary
Force marched into the ambush, the advance team and
he would move to execute the third part of the plan.
They would teleport to Kabul and assassinate the Emir
Abdur Rahman, pinning the blame on the Pathan warlord, Umra Khan.

The Russians would be certain to take advantage of
their "friend" the emir being murdered by a Pathan
warlord. They would march into Kabul and launch a
punitive expedition against the tribes on the frontier,
then not only control Afghanistan, but the British frontier buffer state between Rahman's empire and India. It
would lead to war, and history would be unalterably
changed.

He activated his warp disc and clocked to his camp
headquarters, materializing in his private chambers.
Sadullah fell on his knees before him.

"I have failed, Holy One!" he moaned. "Forgive me!
You have worked wonders to give me the chance to
strike at the *firinghi* once more, and I have failed again.
How can I make amends? How may I redeem my
unworthiness in your eyes?"

"You have failed no one save yourself, Sadullah,"
Drakov told him. "I warned you of this before. I did
not expect for you to succeed at Chakdarra, only to
light the flame of rebellion so that it would burn on
after you had gone. Even now Hadda Mullah carries on

your work. I am not displeased.''

"Oh, bless you, Holy One! Truly, you are the most charitable and forgiving of—''

"Charitable?'' said Drakov. "Forgiving? Let me show you how forgiving I am.''

He beckoned Sadullah forward. The mullah followed him to one of the towers of the house, the entrance to which was barred by a heavy door. Drakov unlocked it. "In here,'' he said, "you will see the price of failure.''

He swept his arm out to indicate that Sadullah should ascend the stairs. Fearfully the mullah went through the door and slowly climbed the stairs. Drakov waited down below. He did not have long to wait. Moments later, a shrill throat-rending scream came from the tower.

Sadullah had climbed to the top of the tower, where he saw himself. Knowing nothing of Zen physics, he did not understand that he, who had been brought from the alternate timeline where he had already lost his holy war, now confronted his own twin in this timeline, whose place he had taken. He only saw himself, staked out naked on the floor, dying the Death of a Thousand Cuts.

The man Sadullah saw was beyond reason. He had been kept alive for weeks, given only bread and water to sustain him while slowly, over a period of time, Drakov's guards had made hundreds of small incisions in his skin, pushing in the thorns while the wounds were still raw and bleeding.

Those wounds now festered with infection. The gangrenous skin was turning mottled green and black. Flies covered the filthy, scrofulous body, which despite it all was still alive. Lice crawled in the long, matted white hair. The eyes, protruding from their hollowed sockets, stared blankly at the ceiling, seeing nothing. Bilious spittle ran out of the corners of the mouth and maggots writhed in the infected wounds.

The screams from the top of the tower continued unabated. Drakov smiled. After seeing that, the mullah would risk anything, even death in battle, to avoid that fate. Sadullah would not fail now.

"What an extraordinary adventure!" Churchill said. "Attacked by Ghazis, escaping, and then traveling all alone through miles of hostile territory to find safe haven with the regiment. Incredible. I will be sure to mention it in my dispatches. What a sterling example of indomitable English spirit!"

"If it's all the same with you, Winston, I'd rather you not mention it at all," said Andre. "A story such as that would only result in notoriety when I returned to England. I really have no wish to be deluged by requests to lecture upon my 'harrowing adventures in Afghanistan.' Nor would I wish to be known as an adventuress. I would much prefer to enjoy my privacy."

Churchill nodded. "Yes, well, certainly, since you put it that way, I quite understand. I will accede to your wishes. There is no lack of things to write about. We have had ourselves quite a time since we departed the Malakand fort. I said earlier that you had found safe haven here, but I must admit I do not quite know how safe it is. We have had reports the camp will be attacked tonight."

"Tonight?" said Finn. "Where did this intelligence come from?"

"The khan of Nawagai has informed us so. He states that he has 'definite information' that a determined assault will take place tonight. I shouldn't be surprised. He will play both ends against the middle until he sees how it all comes out, whereupon he will give his allegiance to the victor. The politics of expediency seem to be a way of life with the tribes on the frontier. Friends one day, enemies the next, one battle decides the outcome and then the next is approached afresh." He chuckled. "Much like the House of Commons, in a way."

"How does General Blood plan to deal with this threatened attack?" said Andre.

Churchill shrugged. "There are no alternatives except to make a stand. Retreat in such uncertain political circumstances would be unthinkable. We must hold our position until General Elles arrives. The pass must be kept open, the khan 'expediently' loyal. And the Hadda Mullah's Ghazis must not, under any circumstances, be permitted to join with the tribesmen of the Mamund. Therefore we are entrenched, a bold course, but soundly conceived. Our position is commanded by the surrounding heights, but unlike the Malakand, in this case the range is long. If an attack is launched, orders are to strike our tents, and all those not employed in the trenches must lie down, thereby reducing the risk of casualties. If they attack in force, we stand and fight.

"We expected an attack last night, but only a half-hearted attempt was made, one easily repulsed. We lost one man. Prior to that there had been some skirmishing. The squadron lost one horse when Ghazis opened fire on us from a nullah, and that night one fool who strayed some fifty yards from his picket was killed by tribesmen lurking in the dark. It's astonishing that you were able to get through. The enemy is always out there, creeping close at night and sniping or trying to kill the pickets. Everyone's nerves are a bit on edge. You were fortunate. If you had come just one half hour later, you would most certainly have encountered savages taking advantage of the dark to get in close. They're building up to it, that much is certain. Tonight may well be the night. I'm looking forward to it."

"I don't think I am," Andre said.

"Never fear, Miss Cross. I shall keep close to you.

You have had quite an ordeal, but it shall be over soon. Once the pass is forced, we will have broken their resistance. After that it will only be a matter of destroying the fortified villages and bringing them to complete submission.''

''I hope you're right,'' said Andre.

Shots cracked out in the night. Churchill paused to listen. ''More sniping?'' he said. ''Or could this be the push?''

Further shots followed rapidly, and the answer came when the order to strike the tents was passed. The men took to the trenches while others lay flat on the ground, protected by the entrenchment walls, but there was still danger from the dropping bullets. The soldiers conserved their fire. There was nothing to shoot at, no definite targets in the darkness. No one walked unless it was absolutely imperative, and even then they did so at great risk.

''Somewhat ignoble way to spend the evening, don't you think?'' said Churchill, keeping his head low to the ground.

''I was tired anyway,'' said Finn. ''I needed to lie down.''

Churchill's chuckle was lost in the screaming of the Ghazis who suddenly came charging out of the darkness on all sides of the camp. Volley after volley was poured into them and still they came, waving their swords, charging right into the bayonets of the troops. The new magazine rifles, coupled with the lethal dumdum bullets, took their toll as Ghazis fell by the dozens. There was no panic. The soldiers maintained disciplined fire in the face of a frightening onslaught, and the big guns fired star shells to illuminate the field in a pale, surreal light.

For those lying on the ground, well behind the trenches, there was nothing to do but remain flat and hope a stray bullet would not find them. Only Finn and Andre had a great deal more occupying their attention. They had to keep constantly on the alert for anyone approaching. The first charge was stopped and whistles blew, signaling an end to independent firing. Volley fire was the order now, until another charge threatened to break through.

It was not long in coming. Screaming at the tops of their lungs, the Ghazis came once more, swarming like army ants out of the darkness. Again the devastating fire was resumed. Ghazis charged up to within several yards of the big guns, only to be blown in half when they discharged. The scene in the trenches was a bizarre juxtaposition of men firing while others next to them engaged Ghazis at bayonet point.

Finn and Andre could spare no time to worry about Ghazis. They were watching their own troops, craning their necks all around to see if anyone in a British uniform was moving closer. And then the mortar fire started. The first shell exploded some thirty yards to the left of the camp, taking out more than a dozen Ghazis as it burst. The second one came moments later, striking just in front of the trenches.

Finn leaped on top of Churchill and kept him pinned beneath his weight as bullets whipped past them.

"We've got to find the bastards before they zero in!" yelled Finn. At that moment a bullet struck him in the arm. "I'm hit!"

Churchill struggled to get up, but Finn pressed him down.

"Stay here!" shouted Andre.

Churchill never noticed Andre clocking out. Another shell landed, sending up clouds of dust and clods of earth as it struck the entrenchment wall. Men screamed. The Ghazi attack continued unabated as they charged the trenches again and again and the British soldiers kept up a punishing stream of fire.

Andre took a gamble. She clocked blind, trying to estimate relative distance coordinates for the heights behind the camp. She thought she knew the weapon being used, or its alternate universe equivalent—a pop mortar, a small tubelike weapon fired from the shoulder with scope sights attached on a slender, collapsible stalk. It would be equipped with night sights, and it fired tiny, ball-shaped missiles about the size of walnuts. Its operation was completely silent except for an almost imperceptible popping sound made by the launching of the missles.

The plan was clear now. They had never intended to infiltrate assassins to kill Churchill. Instead they had taken up position on the heights in order to drop well-placed mortar fire into the camp, taking out the big guns and cutting down on the British advantage, allowing the Ghazis to break through. A few more shots and they would be zeroed in, able to drop missiles directly into the trenches.

Andre tried to estimate trajectory, to think as they had thought, to find the most logical place to set up their point of fire. They needed to be well away from the attacking Ghazis, and the best vantage point for the battle were the heights directly behind the encampment, on the side opposite the Bedmanai Pass. She still had to find them quickly, but it left a great deal of territory to search. Unless she was very lucky, the odds of finding them were very small. And that meant Churchill's death—and Finn's.

12 ———————————

Phoenix heard the screams coming from the top of the tower in Drakov's residence. Sayyid Akbar was home again. He felt the molecular disruptor beneath his robe. It gave him a profound feeling of security. He was sure the opposition wouldn't have such weapons. There were only a few in existence, all prototypes made by Darkness. The Temporal Army could not figure out a way to duplicate them. The principles of the weapon's operation had been explained to them in detail, but they just couldn't make one. He could not imagine a duplicate Dr. Darkness in the alternate universe. The thought of two of them was unnerving.

Most of the village was empty now, save for the women and children. The men had all gone to take up their positions in the Khyber Pass, preparing for the ambush of the Tirah Expeditionary Force. Phoenix had remained behind, watching Drakov's residence. He had seen Sadullah going in and knew the attack would not begin without him. He wondered what Drakov was doing to him to instill the terror necessary for absolute obedience.

"Is he inside?"

Phoenix jumped about a foot. The voice had come from about five inches away. He turned to see Darkness standing at his elbow.

"Jesus, Doc, I wish you wouldn't do that. I swear, you're going to give me a heart attack one of these days."

"Don't concern yourself," said Darkness. "I know CPR. You haven't answered my question."

"Yeah, he's in there, all right. Putting the fear of God into old Sadullah. They're ready to move. Where's the expeditionary force?"

"Approaching the pass," said Darkness. "I've found the confluence point, thanks to the adjustment team."

"They're okay?"

"They won't be if I don't get back to help them," Darkness said. "Forrester is ready to move with the First Division on my signal, which I'll give him the moment the soldiers from the alternate timeline start coming through the confluence. After that both they and you are on your own. I must get to the adjustment team and help them stop the second assault upon the timestream."

"The *second* assault?"

"Never mind. It would take too long to explain. We've reached the crisis point. Make your move."

Phoenix was about to reply, but Darkness was already gone. He shook his head, wondering what it must be like to live that way, at light speed. One of these days, thought Phoenix, he'll translate and his tachyons will take off in sixty zillion directions at the same time, and then where will he be? Probably everywhere.

He pulled the disruptor out from beneath his robe and approached the house.

• • •

There was only one way to search for the mortar team and it was risky. She had to change her transition coordinates rapidly, clocking blind from place to place atop the heights overlooking the camp. The task seemed hopeless. There were hundreds of places for them to hide and she had to find them quickly, before their mortar fire turned the tide of the battle. She was desperate. It had all come down to her, and she could not afford to be cautious.

She initiated a warp fugue sequence, one that would allow her to teleport all over the vicinity with lightning speed, but she was afraid it wouldn't be enough. Finn knew what the odds were, yet he had stayed behind to protect Churchill with his life. She couldn't let him down. She couldn't lose him too. If she was wrong, if she hadn't properly estimated their strategy and they were not in the area she was searching, then it was all over.

She effected over thirty transitions with incredible speed, but they had already found their range and their fire was now falling into the camp with telling effect. The Ghazis, doubtless believing this was the divine intervention they were promised, renewed their assaults with fanatical determination. She kept estimating possible lines of fire and clocking to those points, all without result. Suddenly they were right in front of her, no more than five feet away.

She reacted quickly, firing from the hip, and the man with the pop mortar became enveloped in the blue mist of the disruptor's neutron beam. She fired again and the second man fell as he was bringing his laser to bear on her, then a jarring impact on her back sent her tumbling to the ground. She dropped the disruptor and wrestled with the man who had tackled her. She jerked aside and the knife scraped along her skull, opening a deep gash in the left side of her head. She trapped the knife hand and rolled on it, disloding her antagonist and reversing their positions. She brought her right hand down hard, fore-knuckle extended, into her opponent's throat, crushing his larynx, then struck again twice more and he lay still. Breathing heavily, she slowly got to her feet and came face to face with Priest, standing about ten feet away, aiming his laser at her.

She froze. Both of them stood there atop a cliff over-looking a raging battle, and neither moved. The laser was leveled directly at her chest, but Priest hesitated. Then he slowly lowered the weapon. She stared at him with disbelief.

He shut his eyes briefly. "Andre, forgive me."

The laser started to come up again, and then it fell from his hands as his entire body jerked forward. The point of a bayonet came through his chest, then with-drew again. He collapsed onto the ground. Finn De-laney stood behind him, blood pouring from the wound in his shoulder and one in his arm. He held a Lee-Metford rifle in his hands, its bayonet wet with blood.

"I saw the beam flashes—" he began, then sank down to his knees, holding onto the rifle for support. She was at his side in an instant.

"How's Churchill?"

"He'll be all right now," said Finn, breathing heav-ily. "The Ghazis broke through to the camp and it was touch and go for a while, but they beat back the assault. I'm beginning to think that Blood's men could subdue the entire frontier all by themselves." He glanced down at the corpse. "It's a good thing I didn't have to see his face."

"I see I wasn't needed," Darkness said.

They looked up to find him standing in front of them. He wasn't entirely substantial. The stars in the night sky could be seen through his body and he seemed to shimmer in the dark. He looked exhausted.

"You two look a mess," he said.

"How did you find us?" Andre said.

"I had to search the entire surrounding area at light speed," Darkness said. "I was still too late, wasn't I? I'm getting too old for this sort of thing. I'm a doctor, for Christ's sake, not a commando. Remind me to give you both symbiotracers so I won't have to search all over creation everytime the two of you get into a jam. I need to go home and rest."

"What's happening in the pass?" said Finn.

"I've done all I can. The rest is up to Forrester and Phoenix."

"Phoenix?" said Andre. "Who's Phoenix?"

But Darkness was already gone.

The pipes of the Gordon Highlanders could be heard skirling in the distance as the Tirah Expeditionary Force came through the Khyber Pass. Learoyd, Ortheris, and Mulvaney stood upon the parapet of their cell, looking out into the distance, where they could see the well-formed lines of the British troops advancing.

"They're marching right into a trap," Learoyd said, "and we're helpless to do anything to warn them!"

"Bloody Ghazis mean for us to see 'em cut to ribbons, an' then they'll come back an' take care of us," said Ortheris.

Behind them they heard the bolt to the cell door being drawn back.

"Right," said Mulvaney. "It's all or nothin', lads. Let's show these 'eathens what fightin' men are made of!"

They ran down to the door and as it opened, grabbed the tribesman who came through, and twisted the rifle out of his hands.

"No, Sahib! No!"

"Christ!" said Mulvaney. "It's Din!"

"Good ol' Din," said Ortheris. "Look 'ere, he's done a couple of 'em what for!"

Two dead tribesmen lay in the corridor outside. Gunga Din opened his robe and produced several knives and pistols, then took the rifles away from the two dead tribesmen.

"You use these, yes?" he said. "We fight well, save soldiers!"

"Bless your 'eart, Din," said Mulvaney. "We'll fight 'em, all right."

"We'll never get to them in time," Learoyd said. "They'll spring the trap and our lads will be caught in a crossfire before we can ever break free of this blasted temple!"

Din ran up the steps to the parapet and looked down. He could see the troops below, marching in formation, and above them in the rocks on both sides of the pass, white robed Ghazis waiting for the signal to spring their trap. He reached into the folds of his robe and pulled out his battered bugle. He raised it to his lips and sounded Retreat.

The shrill notes of the bugle call echoed in the pass, and the bagpipes stopped their playing. Din inhaled deeply and blew again.

The door to the cell burst open and armed tribesmen burst through. Mulvaney shot one down, then clubbed another with his rifle. Learoyd crossed knives with one; the two sword-like blades filled the cell with a clanging counterpoint to the bugle call. Ortheris brought two tribesmen down with his pistol, but still more came running into the cell.

"Blow, Din!" yelled Learoyd. "Blow for all you're worth, soldier!"

Din heard Learoyd call him *soldier* and his face broke

into a wide grin. He raised the bugle to his lips once more and played with all his heart. Then the first bullet took him in the back. Several of the tribesmen who had broken into the cell had raised their rifles and fired at him again and again. Learoyd cut one down, Ortheris shot another, but Din took at least five more bullets before Mulvaney threw himself bodily against the other riflemen and forced the door shut, leaning against it and holding it closed with all his might. Ortheris joined him to lend his weight to the door.

Gunga Din sounded three more pathetic, broken notes then fell forward, draped over the wall of the parapet. Learoyd reached him just in time to save him from going over. He pulled him back and laid him gently on the floor. Din's back and chest were a bloody ruin. Blood frothed his lips. He stared up at Learoyd and smiled.

"Din do well, Sahib?"

The troops below had dispersed and taken cover as the Ghazis started firing indiscriminately. It would be a long and drawn-out battle, but their ambush had failed. Learoyd looked down at Gunga Din, his lips drawn tight.

"You did well, soldier. You did damn bloody well."

He saluted him.

Din coughed twice and attempted to raise his own hand to return the salute, but it fell back lifelessly onto the floor.

"You're a better man than I am, Gunga Din," Learoyd said softly. He reached forward and closed the Hindu's sightless eyes.

There was a knock at the cell door. Mulvaney and Ortheris, leaning all their combined weight against it, stared at each other.

"Who's there?" said Ortheris.

"What do you mean, who's there?" Mulvaney said. "Who in bloody 'Ell d'you *think* is there, you stupid sod?"

"You just can't help some people," Finn's voice came from the other side of the door. "You get 'em out of trouble, and like idiots they go barging right back in."

"Blimey!" said Mulvaney. They opened the door and saw Finn and Andre standing amidst a pile of Ghazi corpses.

"You boys ready to leave now?" said Finn. "Or were you planning on setting up housekeeping?"

"You're wounded, sir," said Ortheris. "And you, Miss Cross!"

"It isn't serious," said Andre. "Come on, we'd better get you out of here."

"Holy jumping Christ!" Learoyd shouted from the parapet. "Take a look at this!"

Below and to their left, around the bend of the pass, a wild battle was raging between the Ghazis and the British troops. Below and to their right, armed men clad in field-gray uniforms began appearing as if from out of nowhere, materializing out of thin air. The moment they started coming through, Forrester's division, hidden in the rocks above, opened fire. The pass below them became a deadly latticework of laser beams.

"I must be dreamin'," said Mulvaney, looking down. "What in God's name is goin' on down there?"

Ortheris was speechless. He could only stare, slack-jawed, at a sight he couldn't comprehend. The troops from the alternate timeline didn't stand a chance. Forrester had employed the same tactics against them that the Ghazis had hoped to use against the British troops, and the gray-uniformed soldiers could only ineffectually return the fire sporadically as they came through and died. Then, suddenly, the men stopped coming through.

Stability had been restored to the scenario and the rippling effect moved on. The confluence point shifted and those caught coming through at that precise instant screamed as they were caught between the timelines, materializing momentarily only to disappear again, trapped forever in the limbo of non-specific time known as the dead zone. It hadn't lasted more than several minutes. Forrester's men ceased fire while just out of sight, around the bend in the pass, the echoing thunder of rifle shots continued as the British engaged the Ghazis.

"What did we just see, lads?" said Learoyd. "What in the name of heaven were all those lights? Who were those men?"

"What men?" said Finn.

"What lights?" said Andre.

Learoyd turned to look at them, dumbfounded. "But you were standin' right here! Surely you saw them?"

"Saw who?" said Finn. "Learoyd, what are you talking about? Are you all right?"

"It must have been the strain," said Andre.

"Strain!" said Learoyd. "Mulvaney, *you* tell them! You saw it!"

Mulvaney looked from Learoyd to Finn and Andre. "Saw what, Chris?"

"Those lights! Those men!"

Mulvaney licked his lips. "I didn't see no lights, mate."

"You lying . . . Stanley! You saw it, didn't you? You must have seen it!"

Ortheris looked away guiltily.

"Come on, Chris," said Andre, holding out her hand to him. "It'll be all right. It's over now."

Learoyd looked from Mulvaney to Ortheris to Finn and Andre, then drew himself up. "Right. Fine. It was all a bloody hallucination then, was it? A damned mi-

rage? We didn't see a bloomin' thing, right? Right.
Fine. Splendid. Let's get the hell out of here.''

Phoenix didn't waste any time. He killed the guards
in front of Drakov's headquarters and moved fast, running across the courtyard and into the main house. He
was dressed like a Ghazi, so the women in the main
chamber paid him no mind as he headed for the upstairs
section. He met Sadullah coming down the stairs, but
the mullah took no notice of him. His face was as white
as his hair as he hurried to the scene of battle.

Phoenix took the stairs two at a time. He peered
cautiously around the corner, looking into the main
room on the second floor. There was nothing there except for the opulent furnishings, the tapestries and the
thick rugs and the cushions. He glanced at the balcony
facing out over the pass and saw Drakov standing there,
his back to him. He took aim with his disruptor and
fired.

The figure on the balcony became briefly enveloped
in blue mist and then was gone. Phoenix walked into the
room and suddenly felt powerful arms around him. The
disruptor was twisted from his grasp and he was thrown
to the floor. Drakov stood behind him, wearing the
clothes of one of his guards.

"I knew you'd be back for me, Martingale," he said.
"Or is that really your name? You were with them all
along, weren't you? Right from the beginning."

"It's over, Nikolai," said Phoenix. "Your people
have lost."

"I expected as much when I didn't find any of them
at the temple," Drakov said. "And when Priest did not
contact me, I guessed that you had somehow foiled his
attempt on Churchill's life, as well. And that means the
entire plan's collapsed. No point in going on. They
underestimated you, but they won't do so again. It isn't

over. The war has only just begun."

"What's in it for you, Nikolai? They're not your people. You belong in this timeline."

Drakov shook his head. "I do not belong anywhere," he said. "I must make my own world and find a place in it. And through this new conflict, I shall succeed. You are a survivor, Martingale, but then, so am I. We could have accomplished unimaginable things together, but you chose to serve the enemy instead. So be it. We shall see which of us survives in the end. Meanwhile the game continues."

With a smile he threw the disruptor on the floor in front of Phoenix, and before the startled agent could react, Drakov had clocked out.

"Son a bitch," said Phoenix. "He's out of his fucking mind, but the bastard's got style."

He picked up the disruptor and made a thorough search of the house, destroying whatever modern weapons and equipment he could find. He discovered a hideous thing in the tower and put it out of its misery. Then, having done all he could think of doing, he took one last look around at the year 1897 and went home.

The attack on Blood's brigade lasted for six hours. The British soldiers held and the Ghazis finally retired before the devastating, superior firepower of the troops. The losses among the British were astonishingly slight, considering the ferocity of the onslaught. The most serious losses were among the horses and transport animals. The Ghazis left behind over 700 corpses. General Elles arrived with his brigade the following day, and the Bedmanai Pass was forced. The rebellion in the northern sector of the frontier was broken.

Winston Churchill never discovered what became of Finn Delaney and Andre Cross. One moment they were both pinning him down to the ground, the next they were gone without a trace. He searched for them and made inquiries, but they were nowhere to be found and it was assumed that they were carried off and killed by Ghazis. Their bodies were never recovered. Churchill was tempted to mention them both in his dispatches, but two things prevented him from doing so. One was that he recalled the promise he had made to Andre Cross to respect her privacy; the other was that it was later discovered there was no subaltern by the name of Finn Delaney on the lists. It was suspected that he had committed some sort of crime and had assumed a new identity in order to escape its consequences. The officers of Blood's brigade agreed that whoever and whatever else he might have been, the man they knew as Finn Delaney died a hero.

General Lockhart defeated the forces of Sayyid Akbar after a fierce battle and continued on with the Tirah Expeditionary Force to crush the uprising of the Pathans. He brought the tribes to their knees and they submitted, surrendering their weapons and paying the fines the British Raj imposed. Sayyid Akbar was never found. Sadullah, likewise, had escaped. The swift action of a specially formed Search and Retrieve Unit from the 27th century prevented the British troops from discovering the bodies of soldiers wearing strange gray uniforms and carrying weapons that would have defied any explanation. The confluence point had shifted, and in that period of history at least, temporal stability had been restored.

Privates Learoyd, Ortheris, and Mulvaney were decorated for bravery, and a special, posthumous decoration was given to the Hindu *bhisti*, Gunga Din. He was buried as a British soldier, with full military honors. None of the three of them ever mentioned seeing anything unusual in the Khyber Pass, although when Mulvaney got drunk, he was sometimes heard to mumble about "them bloody lights." None of them ever mentioned an officer named Finn Delaney either. Before Finn left them to "escort Andre back to Peshawar and on her return journey to England," he "confessed" to them that he was a deserter, wanted for a certain crime, and that it would be best for him if they did not mention his name. As men who were well-known for not being overfond of regulations, the three soldiers agreed to keep the secret. The only inquiries ever conducted were those made by Chris Learoyd on his return to England. He made a determined effort to locate a young woman named Miss Andre Cross, but he never found her.

EPILOGUE ═══════════════

The services were held for Major Lucas Priest in front of the Wall of Honor, where his name had been added to the list of those members of the First Division who had died in combat. The entire division had turned out in full dress, and Forrester, wearing his many decorations, delivered the eulogy. Director General Vargas was present and he awarded Priest a posthumous decoration, the Medal of Honor, the oldest and highest award a soldier could receive. At the close of the service, Forrester called the men to attention and Director General Vargas came forward to address them.

"Stand at ease," he said. "A solemn occasion such as this may not be the best time for this briefing, but we are faced with a new and very serious threat. I leave from here tonight to go directly to the meeting of the Council of Nations in Geneva. As of this morning, an official ceasefire was called in all current temporal confrontation actions. I have been in contact with the Council members separately and we have been conducting informal negotiations. I have no reason to believe there will be any dissension during the session of the Council.

"The scientific evidence I will present at the session is overwhelming in its conclusiveness. We are faced with a confluence effect between two separate timelines, an effect rendering both timestreams unstable. Due to unthinking and tragic actions on our part, we have been confronted with hostile actions from the other timeline. There is, at present, no means of negotiating with the opposition and no reliable means of pinpointing the various loci of confluence. Every effort will be made to pursue that course, but in the meantime we must be prepared to face further hostilities, further attempts at interfering with our history in order to cause a temporal split in our own timestream.

"For this reason a massive and rapid reorganization of our temporal forces and support apparatus is essential, and these changes are already under way. In order to meet this new threat, the Referee Corps has decided to merge the two units most experienced in temporal confrontation and adjustment actions. As of this moment, officially, the Temporal Intelligence Agency has been brought under the umbrella of the Temporal Army Command, and I will propose at the Council of Nations meeting that we establish a unified command among all temporal forces, to be headquartered here at Pendleton Base. Henceforth the quasi-civilian status of the TIA is converted to full military status, with an end to the covert nature of their activity in this timeline. The function of monitoring temporal inconsistencies and disruptions will be taken over by the Observer Corps.

"The First Division is henceforth incorporated into the TIA and Colonel Forrester is assigned as deputy director with the rank of brigadier-general. This new unit will be headquartered here, and additional quarters will be provided for the new incoming personnel. Special security procedures will be devised to guard against in-

filtration. The function of this new agency will be
twofold: to conduct adjustment operations to maintain
temporal integrity, and to conduct active, covert operations to create disruptions in the alternate timeline if
points of confluence for crossover can be identified.
You will be briefed as developments occur. In the meantime all leaves are cancelled and the entire unit is on
Yellow Alert standby status. General Forrester?"

Forrester called the unit to attention.

"There remains one more item of buisness which I
would like to personally take care of before I depart for
the Council meeting," Vargas said. "Lieutenant Finn
Delaney and Sergeant Andre Cross, step forward
please."

They marched to the front and stood to attention.

"I would like to personally commend you on your
performance," Vargas said. He stepped forward and
pinned the Temporal Star on both of them, then handed
each of them a small plastic box containing insignia of
rank. Andre was promoted to the rank of second lieutenant and Delaney, to his chagrin, found himself looking down at captain's bars. As Vargas gave him the
bars, he smiled. "Try not to strike anyone above the
rank of major, Captain," he said. "We need capable
officers such as yourself."

After Forrester dismissed the unit, most of them ad-
journed to the First Division lounge, where they all
made a final toast to Lucas Priest. Forrester joined Finn
and Andre at their table.

"I'm buying," he said. "I don't know about you
two, but I'm in a mood to get blind drunk."

"Sounds good to me," Delaney said. Andre nodded.
Forrester cracked a bottle and poured for them. "To
Lucas," Finn said.

They raised their glasses.

"I'd like to join in that toast, if I may," said a voice from behind them.

They turned to see a colonel dressed in black base fatigues standing behind them. His sandy hair was cropped short and his gray eyes regarded them steadily with a somber expression.

Finn almost dropped his glass. "Martingale! But . . . you're supposed to be dead!"

"No, just transferred." He came to attention and saluted Forrester. "Colonel Steiger reporting for duty, sir."

Forrester returned his salute absently and beckoned him to sit.

"Steiger?" Andre said.

"It's my real name. Now that the TIA has gone army, we've dispensed with code names and agent Phoenix is now just plain Colonel Creed Steiger."

"Phoenix!" Finn said. "So you're the one Darkness was talking about."

Steiger nodded. "By the way, he asked me to give you these."

He held out two small plastic envelopes containing what looked like plastiskin grafts.

"Symbiotracers?" Andre said.

"He thought they might come in handy." Steiger looked over his shoulder and they followed his gaze. There was a strange dark blur in the far corner of the First Division lounge, and as they watched, it resolved itself into the figure of Dr. Darkness. He held a glass of scotch whiskey in his hand. "About that toast," said Steiger.

"To Lucas," Finn repeated.

"To Lucas."

They raised their glasses and drank. When they looked back, Darkness was gone.

AUTHOR'S NOTE ═══════════

Although the historical events portrayed in this book actually happened (with the exception of my embellishments, of course), certain events were compressed and sequentially altered for the sake of the story. Winston Churchill obtained six weeks of leave from his regiment and arrived at Malakand on September 2nd of that year in the capacity of press correspondent for the *Pioneer* and *Daily Telegraph*. He was anxious to see active service and wanted to be eventually attached to the force in a military capacity. Consequently his actual arrival on the scene took place at a later point than I have it taking place in this story, but he was involved in the campaign and he chronicled in detail the adventures and accomplishments of the Malakand Field Force in a book by the same name, for which I am indebted to the people at The Court Place Bookshop and Fine Arts Galley in Denver.

Sharif Khan (alias agent Phoenix) was, as might be suspected, a fictional creation, but Sadullah the Mad Mullah (believe it or not, I didn't make that up) and

Sayyid Akbar actually existed, as did the British officers who are named. The story of Surgeon-Lieutenant Hugo saving a man's life by holding his severed artery closed with his fingers while under enemy fire for three hours is genuine, and I could not resist including such an incredible feat in my narrative.

Devotees of Rudyard Kipling will naturally recognize Gunga Din, the regimental *bhisti*, as they will be familiar with Learoyd, Ortheris, and Mulvaney, who appeared in *Plain Tales from the Hills* and *Soldiers Three*. And if you haven't read any Kipling, may I earnestly urge you to acquaint yourself with one of the world's greatest storytellers. Those interested in the history behind this story can find a great deal of available information in their local library, and I especially recommend Charles Miller's *Khyber: British India's Northwest Frontier*, for having a highly readable and entertaining style.

I am also indebted to Bill Barr and to John J. Harty for providing me with information about jezail rifles. Acknowledgments must also be given to those who, in one way or another, provided valuable support during the writing of this book: Leanne Christine Harper and Chuck Rozanski of Mile High Comics in Denver, Colorado; Edward Bryant; Robert M. Powers; the Denver Area Science Fiction Association; and Ginjer Buchanan of the Berkley Publishing Group.

And, of course, special thanks to Dr. Darkness for general wizardry and special effects.

Simon Hawke
Denver, Colorado